WILLIE AND THE RATTLESNAKE KING

Also by
Clara Gillow Clark

ANNIE'S CHOICE

NELLIE BISHOP

WILLIE AND THE RATTLESNAKE KING

Clara Gillow Clark

Boyds Mills Press

Text copyright © 1997 by Clara Gillow Clark
All rights reserved

Published by Caroline House
Boyds Mills Press
815 Church Street
Honesdale, Pennsylvania 18431
Printed in the United States of America

Publisher Cataloging-in Publication Data
Clark, Clara Gillow.
    Willie and the rattlesnake king / by Clara Gillow Clark. – 1st ed.
[196]p. : col.ill. ; cm.
Summary:A thirteen-year-old boy learns life's lessons when he runs
away from the farm to join a traveling medicine show.
ISBN 1-56397-763-X
1. Adolescence–Fiction–Juvenile literature. 2. Runaway
teenagers–Fiction–Juvenile literature. [1. Adolescence–Fiction.
2. Runaway teenagers–Fiction.] I. Title.
813.54 [F]–dc20   1997   AC   CIP
Library of Congress Catalog Card Number 96-80400

First Boyds Mills Press paperback edition,1999
Book designed by Tim Gillner
The text of this book is set in 12-point Veljovic Medium.

10 9 8 7 6 5 4 3 2 1

ACKNOWLEDGMENTS

With gratitude I acknowledge the help and support of the following people. Willie Bishop is a fictional character, but his story is based on people and events of the late 1800s.

My mother, Naomi Keesler Gillow (granddaughter of Nellie Bishop Martin and Jefferson Martin); Alice Minckler Gillow (great-granddaughter of Abraham Minckler, the Rattlesnake Man); Jon Lowris of the Pocono Snake and Animal Farm, East Stroudsburg, Pennsylvania; The Equinunk Historical Society, Equinunk, Pennsylvania, for its many and fine publications of local and regional history; Jeanne Decker of the Read Memorial Library, Hancock, New York; Doris Davis of the Hancock-Chehocton Historical Society, Hancock, New York; Anne Parsons of the Deposit Free Library, Deposit, New York; Ruth Axtel of the Deposit Community Historical Society, Deposit, New York; Marjory Barnum Hinman of the Broome County Historical Society, Roberson Center, Binghamton, New York; and Gerald R. Smith of the Broome County Public Library, Binghamton, New York.

With love for my son, J. Jay

My name is Willie I am not like Rose.
I would be Willie whatever arose,
I would be Willie if Henry was my name.
I would be Willie always Willie all the same.

—Gertrude Stein, *The World Is Round*

CHAPTER 1

Swish, swisha, swish. The blade of Willie's scythe sounded in the tall grass of the meadow. *Swish, swisha, swish.* He worked steadily, the sweat gathering on his forehead under the brim of his straw hat and trickling down his face. The fingers of the June sun clenched the earth and squeezed the life out of everything. Even the birds and insects had ceased their chatter.

Willie paused and swiped his sleeve over his face. He stared across the field at Jefferson, his sister's husband. The man seemed tireless—the swinging arc of his arm, the swaying of his body—never faltering in his rhythm as he mowed down the grass. How did he do it? Was it the Indian in him? Or was it something else?

Willie and Jeff had started cutting at opposite ends of the field. They planned to meet in the middle of the plot, but as in every blessed thing—it seemed to Willie—Jeff ended up doing more than his portion. Jeff did it good-heartedly, and the extra wasn't done to make Willie look bad. It was just his way, and always had been, even from the beginning when he'd taken Willie and Nellie in two years ago, that June of 1886. Jeff had brought them to his farm a full day's journey from Dyberry Forks, where they used to live. Jeff's family lived in the sparsely settled hills of northern Pennsylvania, miles from even the nearest small village on the Delaware River.

Willie swallowed hard against a sudden queasiness washing over him and held the scythe more tightly as he struggled to keep his legs from buckling. He began hacking at the grass again, watching as large tufts of it fell at his feet. He hated this time of day, when the high sun turned his shadow into a dark puddle at his feet. It made him feel even smaller than he was. He'd be thirteen soon enough, and Nellie was still saying how much he'd grown from the good food and clean air, how he didn't have to roll up his cuffs now, how he'd soon have men's britches. It was true. But he didn't *feel* bigger or older, not a bit. Since leaving town, he felt as if a chunk had been chopped out of him somewhere, like the hunks of hay from the field he was mowing.

Oh, he knew it was a good life—"a good, good life," his sister was ever fond of saying as she hummed and went about her chores. Farm life was hard work but good work, and Jeff was a good man.

Didn't she ever think of town? Miss their prowling through the streets at dusk? She must—but she always denied it.

Nellie would shake her head when he questioned her. Miss town? Ma's beatings? Pa's gambling and drunkenness? Miss being hungry? No.

"What about freedom? What about the independence you talked up so much?" he'd ask. "Seems to me you're a Benedict Arnold to your ownself."

Darkness would pass over her eyes, and then they would clear. No. Her answer was always the same. No. This was a good life for her.

What she couldn't seem to catch onto was that this was not the right life for him. He didn't hanker after Ma and Pa, or the canal rowdies bullying him, but he missed Dyberry Forks. He missed the newspapers, the sidewalks, and the saloons crowded with talk and stories. He missed the clang of the blacksmith's hammers, the clatter of buggies, the array of goods in the shops. He missed scavenging for the small, lost belongings of strangers—there weren't nothing out in the hills for a fella to come upon sudden-like—and he missed the train whistle proclaiming its power over space and time. He had given farm life a long, fair trial, but there were just too many dry spells here with nothing exciting ever going on.

That was why he had to run away. The no-good hankering had been growing in his mind sweet and delicious as the raspberries that grew plump and juicy behind the woodshed and made his mouth water at the sight. But lately the hankering had begun to fester like a wood splinter run deep into his flesh. It was an ache now, an ache that throbbed as constant as his heartbeat. Only the goodness of Jeff and his sister's love had kept him here this long, and the thought of hurting them left a bitterness in his mouth like one of those vile bugs that got unnoticed into the berries. He had no doubt he was a sinner, ungrateful and mean-spirited.

He could hear the other scythe in the grass as Jeff began closing in on him. Willie kept his back turned away and his head bent to his work. He knew that if Jeff caught his eye, the man would call out a greeting. Willie could almost see the broad smile on Jeff's smooth, tanned face. He swallowed against the guilt knotting itself in his throat. It was one thing to run away from hunger and beatings—quite another to run from what was good. Why would he look for trouble? What was in him that clamored for it? But he did. The very idea of it made his skin tingle.

Queasiness washed over him again, and he lowered his head under the weight of the sun's hand. He was about to pitch forward when he was grasped firmly by the arm.

"Time to get out of the sun," Jeff said, steadying Willie.

Willie ducked his head and swallowed. The sick feeling passed, but the shame stayed. "Whupped me again," he said, staring at the stubbled ground. The puddle of his shadow had dried up. He could almost see it in the waves of heat being drawn up into the fist of the sun.

Jeff laughed and shook his head. "Time will change that . . . in time you'll be as thick-skinned as our good ox Jake."

Willie nodded and mustered a small grin.

A thoughtful look came into Jeff's eyes. He removed his straw hat and wiped his forehead with the sleeve of his shirt. "Can't say there's any glory in toiling this way, but it's a good life," he said, squinting as he looked closely at Willie. "Don't cut yourself down like this grass here. You're still a young stalk, and a townie to boot."

Jeff's voice was kind, but his words tasted bitter to Willie. *You're still a young stalk, and a townie to boot.* Didn't matter. He didn't want to wait. He wanted to do something now—anything really important—something that Jeff couldn't do. But Jeff was right, he *was* a townie—and Willie could feel town calling his name.

CHAPTER 2

"Jeff! Wil-lie!" At the sound of his sister's voice, Willie turned. Nellie was standing at the edge of the field, a bucket in one hand, her eyes shaded from the glaring sunlight with the other. "Jeff!" she called again.

Jeff waved an arm in greeting. "Hallooo!" he called.

Willie's shoulders slumped, and he raised an arm in a feeble wave. Jeff, always Jeff. Lately she barely gave Willie, her only brother, the time of day. Scarcely noticed he was around except when she had chores for him.

"Isn't she an angel though?" Jeff said proudly.

Willie rolled his eyes and shook his head. Angel? How did Jeff come up with such silly a notion? His sister looked more like a girl playing at being grown-up, the way she'd taken to piling her hair up so it framed her face like a halo, and wearing those long, flowered skirts with aprons.

Jeff started across the field in long strides, and Willie tagged behind. Dang it all, he wasn't ever going to get syrupy over a girl.

Jeff reached Nellie first and took the pail from her hands, but he waited and handed the tin cup brimming with cool water to Willie. "Drink it slow, take it easy now," Jeff said as Willie began to guzzle the water.

The first cold gulp hurt his throat, and he took smaller swallows and watched the pair of them. Jeff doffed his hat and placed it on his bride's head. "Shouldn't be out in this sun without a bonnet, not a delicate flower like you," he said, smiling gently.

Nellie laughed. "What am I to do with you, Jefferson Martin? Can't you leave me a moment's peace?" she said. Her voice was soft, and she touched Jeff's arm as she looked up into his face and caught him with her eyes.

Willie studied his sister over the brim of the cup. Delicate flower? His sister? Why, Nellie was powerful strong and taller than most girls, taller still than him. He shook his head. Maybe he had the same green eyes and honey-colored hair as his sister, but inside they were as different as a polecat and a tabby—he being the polecat.

He finished the drink and pushed the cup over to Jeff. "Here, your turn," he said, but Jeff didn't seem to hear or notice him. Neither one of them did, so he dropped the tin into the bucket and turned away.

Willie started off toward the house, his shoulders slumped. Shucks. He hated it when the two of them got all mushy that way.

Instead of going along the worn path and through

the gate the way they'd come, Willie cut across the field, climbed over the rock wall, and hiked through the dense stand of hemlocks on the north side. Jeff said those hemlocks protected the house from harsh winter winds. The leafy maples and oaks shaded the house in summer and let the sun through in winter. It seemed to Willie that Jeff never did a blessed thing without studying it into some kind of arithmetic lesson.

Willie slowed down when he came into the dooryard. He was sick of lessons—school, home, church—it was more than a body could bear. Running away was the right thing to do, he was sure, but it wouldn't be easy. People would recognize him, know what he was doing if he didn't plan real careful. He would have to figure out what he would say if he saw someone he knew. And he would need money. That was a problem. He would have to steal it from Jeff and his sister. He shook his head. There must be another way, but he couldn't think of one.

Willie stopped just as he got to the porch steps. What was that sound—a tinkling sound, faint and faraway? He turned and walked back across the yard. It was louder, clearer now, and his heartbeat quickened. He dropped his scythe, letting it clatter on the well stone, and ran toward the sweet tinkling of bells.

"Mister Saul! Isaac Saul!" Willie hollered out as he dashed through the barnyard and down the steep, grassy knoll.

When he broke over the rim of the hill, Willie saw

the peddler with a large pack rising above his head and nearly dwarfing him. In one hand he carried a black leather valise, and in the other a walking stick, which he was leaning on heavily as he panted up the hillside.

"Mister Saul, hallo!" Willie called as he bounded up to the peddler.

"And hallo to you, too, young fella," Isaac said, his darkly whiskered face breaking into a wide smile as he handed over his black bag. He paused, still panting from the climb, and then spoke again. "I see you have grown so much since last fall, Willie Bishop. It must be this good mountain air, yes? Perhaps you grow too tall like this big mountain if you do not be careful. Maybe you should pull your hat tighter on," he said, yanking down on the brim of his own hat.

Willie laughed, his ears growing warm with the generous words, but then he wrinkled his brow. "We're about to have our noon meal. You'll stay?" Willie asked anxiously. "Say yes, Mister Saul. Please? I have to talk to you."

"Ja, ja! How clever of me to arrive just now, though I confess," he said, lowering his voice in a conspiring way, "I had to hurry away from the breakfast table to be here." He patted his quite round stomach and squinted up at the high sun. "It is a shame I tell time so poorly!" His eyes crinkled in fun.

Willie laughed aloud at the peddler's joke. Oh, it was so good that Isaac had come just now when

Willie's hunger for town was so great. "Mister Saul?" Willie said, his mood turning serious. "How old would a boy have to be for you to hire him to work at your store in town?"

Isaac studied his face. "Boys that look strong and old enough to work hard and good." Isaac scrubbed a hand over his beard. "Boys who show some whiskers sprouting."

Willie rubbed his fingers over his chin. Hairless as a hog. He swallowed hard and looked away from Isaac's probing eyes.

Isaac cleared his throat. "What stories I have to tell, young man. But what are we waiting for?" Isaac smoothed his mustache and straightened his back. "Lead the way, my good fellow."

CHAPTER 3

Willie ran his finger along the bottom of his bowl and wiped up the strawberry juice that had escaped his biscuit. He kept one eye trained on Isaac. Seemed like Isaac was never going to finish his meal.

At last Isaac pushed back his plate. "My pack, please," he said. And as the pack was opened, it was as if a little bit of town spilled into the room. Willie had to admit, though only to himself, that in a way this was better than town, because Isaac seemed to understand that a body needed to touch things. The shopkeepers in Dyberry Forks were more wary, at times even shooing him from the front of their store windows if he tarried too long.

"Go ahead, young Willie," Isaac said now. "Whatever you like, pick it up. See if it is good."

Willie gave a long, low whistle. He hovered over the goods but didn't know what to pick up first. There were watches and knives and mouth organs and leather diaries—he wanted them all.

And Jeff said, "Pick yourself something. Anything you'd like, Willie. You've worked plenty hard and you deserve a little something extra."

Willie wet his lips, and his eyes fastened on the tabletop of notions. He swallowed hard. He shouldn't be taking anything from Jeff, and not anything so fine as what he was offering. What would Jeff think if he knew what lurked in Willie's mind?

"Go ahead, get yourself something," Jeff said, smiling. "Never known you to be shy of gadgets afore."

Willie could feel himself weakening, melting down into nothing just like his shadow at noon. What would it hurt just to pick something up? He wouldn't have to take it. He chose a diary and opened it. Inside was a calendar for the year; on the facing page were astronomical calculations—eclipses, phases of the moon, movable feasts, chronological cycles. Other pages held charts of populations of states and principal cities, the distance between New York City and other cities in the United States, rates of postage for postcards, letters, and packages—all sorts of important things for him to know.

Jeff had a diary like this. Willie had peeked in it once, but Jeff only kept a list of the daily chores they had done—nothing exciting, nothing important. If he had a diary, he knew he would write about important things—like train robberies, murders, hangings, tragic deaths, floods, fires, hurricanes . . . He riffled through the pages, then slowly put it back. Someday, when he had something exciting to write about, he would get a diary.

Willie eyed the knives again—there was that one

with a handle rough like tree bark, another with inlaid pearl that a gentleman in town like Mr. Rockwell might fancy. What sort of knife would be right?

Willie picked up the pearl-handled pocketknife. It was smooth and fit nicely in his palm.

"Try it on a stick of kindling," Isaac said. They were all smiling, eager, wanting him to be pleased.

He shouldn't take the knife, not when he was planning to run off. But he *would* need one—and it was better to have his own than to steal from Jeff. Willie pulled open the knife blade. How it shone without a bit of rust! How could any fella pass up such a beauty? He went to the woodbox and grabbed up a stick. How easily the blade cut through the wood, slipped right through as easy as if it were slicing bread. Imagine, this could be *his* knife—his very own, not some lost belonging of a stranger. Owned first and only by him.

How could he think of running away? He had to be the most low-down creature, so low-down and sinful he'd practically be crawling on his belly like a rattlesnake, like the old devil hisself.

Willie shook himself. He'd been listening to the Methodists too long. All they thought about was mortal sin and signs from the Lord. Maybe *this* was a sign directing his path: he needed a knife to run away and now he was being offered one.

"This here one, this is the one," Willie said. He snapped the blade shut and slipped the knife into his pocket. "Thankee, Jeff," he said, keeping his eyes lowered.

"No need to thank me, Willie," Jeff said. "But you're welcome all the same."

Willie nodded. He could feel his sister's glance bright with happiness moving between him and Jeff. "It's splendid of you, Jeff," she said.

Willie wrapped his fingers tight around his new treasure. It was payment, fair and square, for the chores he helped out with every day. He'd earned it, and it didn't make him beholden to stay. Still, inside a sickness seeped into his stomach like fog rolling into the valley at dusk.

As Nellie and Jeff discussed prices and purchases with Isaac, their voices seemed to fade into the heat of the afternoon. Willie was vaguely aware that Nellie was picking out fabric and selecting a new kettle, but his mind snapped sharply away from his new pocketknife and his thoughts of running away at the sound of Isaac's voice. "And now I bid you so long till I see you again in the autumn," he said, doing up the last straps of his pack.

Willie wanted to beg him to stay. The time had gone so quickly and surely Isaac had more to tell.

Isaac stood and was about to put on his pack when he stopped. "One thing I forget." He bent down and pulled a rolled-up paper from his boot. "I find this in the village and I say, Isaac, that young Willie Bishop would find this very big thrill. *Ja?*" He nodded to himself as he presented the handbill to Willie.

CHAPTER 4

Willie's hands shook as he unfurled the handbill and smoothed it out on the tabletop. Isaac looked on with pleasure. Willie began to pour over the paper, feeling his skin tingle.

ABRAHAM MINCKLER SHOW

• • • • • • • • • • •

RATTLESNAKE KING EXTRAORDINAIRE

in his death-defying act with
SERPENT DEVILS

• ALSO •

COUNT VONRONSKY

with
BELLE THE DANCING BEAR
WONDER AND KOKO
THE AFRICAN MONKEY SUPREME

Introducing DR. GRANGER'S GINGER BEER
The Magic Elixir with MIRACLE CURATIVE POWERS

• • • • • • • • • • •

Willie grabbed the handbill and gripped it in both hands. This was surely a sign—a sign so powerful he could scarcely take it in. "Mister Saul, when is the show?" Willie asked anxiously, firing off his words like the report of rifle. "How soon? Where at?"

"Soon, young Willie. Quick enough for you, I reckon." Isaac bobbed his head. "This Saturday, in Equinunk, down on the flats below the church. With a box social and all. And, the ladies . . . ah, the ladies," he said, putting a hand over his heart and letting out a tremendous sigh. "All trying to outdo one another in food and finery."

Willie laughed and shuffled his feet on the rough wood floor. "My feet are itching to go," he cried, but then he caught a glimpse of Nellie. She was paying him no mind as she draped the folds of new calico over her arm and smoothed it with her hand. It was plain enough what she thought of the upcoming show, with her lips pressed together as if biting back words. Willie shifted his eyes toward Jeff expecting the same, but Jeff was rubbing his chin thoughtfully—and there was that quiet studying air about him that the man gave to everything. This was an encouraging sign.

"Jeff, might we go? I'll get up even earlier to do the barn chores and . . . and . . ."

"Slow down, Willie boy," Jeff said, laughing. "No need for that. We'll have time for regular chores and can still take part in the festivities."

Ha! For once Jeff was on *his* side. Willie looked at his sister to see what she thought of that, but her head was bent. She didn't seem to want them to go. That was just like her—never wanting him to have a good time, always set on having her own way. . . . Jeff was leaning over to her now, and Willie held his breath and waited. Jeff would put her in her place.

But Jeff didn't. Instead, he lifted her chin and cupped her face with his hands. "Now don't fret, you're finer than any one of them and lovelier."

She blushed and turned her face away from them. "I . . . I . . . don't think so," she said, biting her lip.

Willie was about to agree, but Isaac spoke up. "*Ja, ja*, it is truth, Nellie. Go, go and see for yourself."

Jeff moved his hands to her shoulders. "You just take whatever time you need to make this calico into a new dress, and Willie and I will help out with the housework so you can. Won't we?"

Willie nodded. "I'll do whatever you say, Nellie." He truly didn't mind helping, if it meant he could go. But he was amazed at the exchange between Jeff and Nellie.

He felt as if he hardly knew Nellie at all these days. But Jeff seemed to. He'd stepped right up to her like a western hero. . . . Willie swallowed hard and turned away.

He felt a hand on his shoulder. It was Isaac. "Willie boy, perhaps you would walk with me to the next farm?"

"Can I go, Jeff?" Willie asked, unable to look at his sister. "Can I show this to Dorrie and the rest?" He folded the handbill and stuffed it carefully down his boot.

"Go ahead," Jeff said, nodding.

Willie felt his cheeks redden. Quickly, he yanked on his hat and reached over to help Isaac with his satchel. Willie groaned inwardly as he fingered his new pocketknife. He felt as if a war was being waged inside of him, and he was powerless to choose sides.

CHAPTER 5

Already the shadows were growing tall as Willie set off with Isaac across the meadow toward the woods that divided Jeff's farm from his folks' place. A few clouds had formed in the sky, and a slight breeze stirred. The afternoon sun had loosened its grip on the day, and the bells on Isaac's pack tinkled happily as the two walked along.

Willie wet his lips. There was so much he needed to know, so little he could ask without causing suspicion. "Um . . . Mister Saul." Willie wrinkled his brow. "That rattlesnake man must be as brave as a soldier, capturing snakes and all."

Isaac laughed. "There's different kinds of bravery, Willie boy. One kind of bravery is what Abe Minckler has. Fearless, he is. Old Isaac here, he would run. *Ja*, I would run as quick as a hare."

They had started into the hemlock woods now, and the coolness and fragrance of the firs were a welcome change. Willie removed his straw hat and wiped his forehead. He wanted to be brave in the way Abe was brave. He couldn't imagine any other kind of bravery, and he was disappointed in Isaac for saying so. "What other kind of bravery is there, Mister Saul?"

Isaac stopped on the path to adjust his pack. "Young Willie, you ever heard the story of David and Goliath?"

Willie nodded. He was almost the height of Isaac, and although the peddler's eyes were keenly fixed on him now, the good man ignored Willie's response and proceeded to tell the story.

"David, a young boy like you, went out to fight a strong and big giant who killed many people, a giant who cared nothing for right, only for killing. Now David, he was small but much brave, and he took a sling and some smooth stones, and with one of these stones he slayed the giant Philistine. Now, I say unto you, Willie Bishop, every man meets at least one Goliath in his life. Sometimes he sees this giant, and sometimes the giant hides." Isaac shrugged in his pack and began to move toward the bright light where the forest ended. "Young Willie, you must be brave to face the giant either way, but when the giant is disguised, it takes more than bravery alone."

They were coming out of the forest now, into a clearing. Willie was fuming. He knew the Bible story well enough, but Isaac's version confused his thoughts. He had always liked the idea of a young boy killing a giant, but now there was no time left to question Isaac further about town. The whole walk had been wasted on a silly story that was of no help to him. He jammed on his hat to repel the sun and kicked a stone in the path so that it went hurtling into the pasture bushes.

Isaac laid a hand on Willie's arm. "Young Willie, some time you want to come to town, you visit me, my family. Someday you can work for old Isaac. I train you good, give you good job."

Willie studied the older man's face. "But not now," he said bitterly.

"Ah, Willie, you have great storm brewing inside, no?" Sadly, Isaac shook his head. "You have trouble, lad, you come find Isaac."

Willie nodded and swallowed hard. He moved away from the peddler. He didn't want to wait a couple years until Isaac thought him old enough. He wanted to go now! He looked out across the pasture toward the Martin farm, and there he saw Dorrie, Jeff's youngest sister, running toward them. As suddenly as his dark mood had come, it passed over him.

The Martins' house was teeming with life, the way pasture flowers were swarming with honeybees, and it was a pleasant place to be. Everyone paid attention to him there; no one watched him to see if his mind was bent on other matters, or yammered at him and hovered around and worried him to death with pesky questions as his sister did, or stared at him with a troubled, studied look the way Jeff sometimes did.

"Dorrie!" he shouted as he hurried toward the girl running to meet him. She had the Indian darkness about her—dark eyes, black hair, and warm, brown skin—and she was just his age, the youngest in the family.

She grabbed hold of Willie's free arm and called "Hallo" to Mr. Saul.

"It's grand to see you, Will-lee. What did you get from the peddler? Jeff said he was going to let you pick something, whatever you wanted, he said, on account of you working so hard and all."

Willie bit down on his lip. He was immediately thrown back into his guilt over accepting the gift from Jeff, and the knife seemed to burn right through his pocket into his flesh. He gave a shaky laugh. "Jeff's real good to me, Dorrie. Can't wait to show you what I got."

When Willie got to the house, he helped Isaac set the satchel down on the porch. "Willie, you not forget Isaac's words. You have trouble, you come. *Ja?*" He spoke quickly and quietly.

Before Willie could reply, the grown-ups swarmed around Isaac, chattering excitedly. Willie watched as they disappeared into the house, Isaac's voice trailing back. "Tea? Currant buns? *Ja*, a spot of something would be *gut*."

"I've something else to show you, Dorrie," Willie said, turning to the girl at his elbow. "A real marvel," he whispered. "Something more exciting than a new hair ribbon."

"Will-lee, I have to see what's in the peddler's pack first," Dorrie said, twisting her head to look at the doorway where the last of the grown-ups had just disappeared. "Mister Saul will be opening his pack now. Pa promised me a present when the peddler came. Come on with me. Help me choose," she said, tugging at his sleeve.

Willie scowled. "Leave me alone then," he said meanly.

Dorrie backed away from him. "What stung you, Will-lee Bishop? You act like a bear with a sore head. You don't mean to say that *you* didn't look in the peddler's pack?" She stuck her nose in the air and whirled around.

"Dorrie, wait, I didn't mean . . . please, don't go yet, Dorrie." Willie wanted to say he was sorry, but the words somehow got stuck in his throat as soon as the girl turned back toward him. "I wanted to show you this," he said, taking the paper from his boot and smoothing out the folds in the handbill. "Thought maybe you'd like to come along, since Jeff said we're going."

Dorrie moved so she could see. She wasn't one to hold a grudge nor to be bullied, and he'd gotten her attention now. "A real show! A marvel!" she cried, clapping her hands together. "There hasn't been one in ever so long. It'll be great fun."

Willie folded the paper. "You mean you've been to a show before?"

"A few times we have, in the village . . . and once a real circus," she said, nodding her head.

The show was nothing, then, nothing special

like he had thought, and he didn't want to own up to it being his first—especially since Dorrie had been to a real circus. "I suppose you've seen the rattlesnake man?"

She shook her head. "Pa said he's real amazing. Has no fear at all. It'll be wonderfully scary, don't you think?" she whispered.

"Yes," he said, feeling much better.

"Dorrie," one of her sisters called from the doorway. "Ma says to come and pick out a new hair ribbon and calico for a dress."

"Coming," she called, but turned back to Willie. "When is the show?"

"Saturday."

"Thursday, Friday, then Saturday," she said, counting off on her fingers. "Only two days to go!"

Two days until the show. It seemed almost too long for him to wait.

CHAPTER 6

On Saturday morning the air was hot and still, but quickly enough the white fleecy clouds and a pleasant breeze sweeping in from the northeast broke the tension, and Willie's own discontent of the night before was shattered in the contagious spirit of an outing.

All through morning chores, he could scarcely contain his itchiness to get them done. In his haste, he had knocked over a pail of milk, but Jeff had only smiled and shook his head in understanding. "Got show fever, lad. You'd best slow down. Now that you're getting older, I guess there'll be times when you can take the team to the village for social occasions yourself."

This news was almost too much for Willie, and he spent the rest of the milking going over the true reasons for running away. It wasn't just for excitement or adventure. The real true reason was that he didn't belong here, and this was not the life he wanted.

"When you're done there and washed up, would you walk over to my folks and fetch Dorrie? Wouldn't want her to think we've gone on without her."

"No, sir," Willie said and hurried through the rest of the morning chores. As soon as he had changed into his best clothes, he went through the hemlock forest to fetch Dorrie.

When he came into the clearing, he could see her standing, watching for him from the porch. She didn't run out to meet him this time.

What ailed her? She wasn't mad about the other day still, was she? He walked clear up to the steps without getting so much as a howdy. He stormed onto the porch, and then she came toward him.

"Will-lee," she said, smiling.

Willie stopped mid-stride, and his heart fluttered up wildly like a grouse startled in a thicket. "Dorrie," he said, but her name seemed to stick in his throat and his tongue felt swollen and useless. He took in the blue forget-me-nots dotting her dress and the blue ribbons in her dark hair. "You look . . . you're as pretty as a flower," he stammered.

"Oh, Will-lee," she said, coming to take his arm. He could tell that she was pleased by the way she ducked her head and the way the color rose in her cheeks.

One of her sisters came out on the porch. "Hello, Willie. You won't mind carrying Dorrie's basket for the box social?" she asked, handing him a basket decorated with paper flowers and smelling of warm bread. She looked at his face and smiled. "No stopping in the woods, lad," she said.

He blushed and took the basket without answering. "Come on, Dorrie," he said gruffly, unable to look at either of them. "Jeff's bound to be waiting on us."

Dorrie followed along, babbling excitedly about the day. When they got to the house, Nellie was waiting for them on the porch. "Jeff wants you in the barn," Nellie said, coming down the steps to meet them.

"What . . . what did I do?" he asked, wetting his lips.

Nellie frowned a little. "Why can't you just do what I ask?" she said. She took Dorrie's basket from him and began exclaiming over the paper flowers and Dorrie's new calico.

Willie walked slowly toward the barn. A part of him wished that his brother-in-law would lash out at him in anger for something—anything—just once.

When Willie got to the barn, Jeff was standing just inside the door. He'd already hitched the team to the wagon and was holding the reins in his hand.

"Nellie said you wanted to see me," Willie said.

Jeff nodded. "Hold the reins for me."

Willie stepped forward and took the leather straps in one hand. He studied his brother-in-law's face, but he couldn't tell what the man had on his mind.

Jeff reached into his vest pocket and pulled out a handful of coins and held them out to Willie. "Thought you might want to bid on some girl's basket at the box social." He wrinkled his forehead and shook his head. "A fella does hate to be beholden to another. It sits much better if a fella can pay his own way in the company of others."

"Obliged," Willie said. He could scarcely keep from grabbing the coins. In his head he was putting a black line through the word *money* on his list. He didn't intend to spend a cent.

Jeff dropped the coins into Willie's outstretched hand and laughed. "They'll be selling magic elixir, but don't waste your money on that."

Willie closed his fingers over the coins, and shoved them deep into his pocket. They clinked against the knife. For an instant, Willie froze. Again, he felt caught in this act of betrayal. He had taken the coins without so much as a twinge of guilt. It was true. But now he wouldn't have to steal; Jeff had given him exactly what he needed as if it had been designed by an act of providence. He looked up at Jeff and flashed him his old, winsome grin.

He saw Jeff's chest heave with relief, and the man's face lit with happiness. "Guess we better not keep the women waiting any longer," he said, giving Willie a companionable slap on the back.

"No, sir," Willie said heartily. He felt suddenly very powerful in the knowledge that he could keep his inner feelings hidden. If he could fool Jeff into thinking that all was well, then he could fool anyone.

CHAPTER 7

Willie sat with Dorrie in the back of the wagon with the baskets of food for the box social. Jeff drove the team, and Nellie perched close beside him on the seat.

Willie had been to the village only a few times since he and Nellie had come to live with Jeff. Just before Christmas, Jeff had taken him down to Calder's General Store to purchase gifts. The trees and bushes had stood out sharply in their shivering nakedness, and snow had lain in patches on the frozen ground. Now the lush foliage of woods and thickets blocked Willie's view of farms and fields.

There were many unmarked roads forking off in all directions, and so he tried to take note of anything unusual—a stand of evergreen, a wall laid up in a particular fashion, a stream, an orchard of fruit trees—but everywhere the countryside looked pretty much the same to him. He had never been good at finding his way alone. He should have asked Isaac how he managed to find his way through this mountain wilderness.

When they reached the village, the roads were crowded with wagons and folks walking to the show. Jeff inched their wagon along the wide leafy lane, past Calder's General Store, Farley the Undertakers, the rectory, the Methodist Church, and the graceful homes and picket fences of the wealthier villagers.

"Will-lee, look!" Dorrie tugged at his sleeve. "There's Pearl." She pointed to a wagon ahead of them, her excited voice buzzing in his ear. "And there's Thomas Thorne," she said, lowering her voice. "Do you see him? Do you? He's driving the team."

An unpleasant bitterness roused itself in Willie's stomach. How could he miss Thomas Thorne? Thomas was being a show-off as usual, driving the team while his folks sat on the seat next to him. And wasn't he sitting up tall and proud, looking around, catching sight of people and waving as if he were the king of something? He and Thomas were the same age, the same level in school, but the other boy seemed nearly a man, even had a mustache, and could easily do the work of ten men to hear him tell it.

Willie pretended not to see Thomas, but turned his full attention to the show. He spotted three grandly painted wagons clumped together beneath the tall, thick-limbed sycamores by the river. He became so absorbed in watching the tents for signs of show people that he was taken off guard when Jeff reined to a halt beneath a stand of poplars where wagons and buggies were being tied up.

"Come on, Will-lee." Dorrie tugged at his sleeve. "If we hurry we can get seats up front."

Willie didn't need urging. He fairly dragged Dorrie along to the very center of the front row.

A makeshift stage had been erected with a canvas roof and sides so that it appeared to be an extension of the largest wagon. The stage platform was set low to the ground, and the rows of plank seating were quite near the edge of the stage.

"Will-lee, we have the best seats," Dorrie said, clutching at his arm, leaning her head against him for a moment.

Willie didn't take his eyes off the wagons and scarcely noticed when Dorrie was joined by her chattering friends. But he jumped when a voice behind him spoke. "Well, if it ain't Willy-nilly."

Willie knew the voice, and he turned slowly, blinking in dismay when he saw Thomas Thorne standing over him. Willie tensed and drew back.

"I've been looking all over for you, Willie," Thomas said. He was twiddling a hay stalk between a finger and thumb of one hand. "I knew you'd be saving a place for me."

Willie studied the other boy's face, but it gave nothing away. He shrugged stiffly, his body still tensed, and smiled as warmly as he could. "Why, have a seat, Thorne," he said, patting the empty spot beside him.

"Right kind of you, my friend," Thomas said, bounding lightly over the board. He squeezed himself between Willie and Dorrie, easily pushing them apart. What could he do against a bully like Thomas? Thomas was just one more good reason for him to run away.

CHAPTER 8

A bugle sounded, cymbals crashed, and women moved in a flurry to locate youngsters and husbands and settle in their seats after one last snatch of important gossip. Then even the cry of small children came to a sudden halt, and all was still.

Willie drew in a breath and expelled it slowly as the heavy velvet of the raggedy curtain was jerked apart. Two jugglers appeared dressed in costumes that looked like the American flag. They began slowly, tossing the balls back and forth, popping them from hand to hand in a sluggish motion. They sang songs and told jokes. This was something he could do, Willie decided, studying the movement of their wrists, but no sooner had he mastered this act in his mind when it changed. The balls began snapping furiously, seeming to jump out of control between the two jugglers like popcorn from a hot skillet, and multiplied as if by magic so that try as he might Willie could not count them nor keep his eyes focused on a single one.

As the performers ended with a patriotic song, and the last of the balls plopped safely one by one into the jugglers' hands, there was a burst of applause.

The curtains closed, and while Willie was still clapping, a man with silver hair and a monocle stepped from behind the velvet folds. He wore a well-tailored somber suit as if he were a man of distinction, and he came forward and stood at the very edge of the platform. He raised his arms over the crowd in a gesture bidding quiet. "Good people." His voice was a strong, musical bass. His gaze swept over the crowd and then settled for an instant, Willie was sure, on him. The man seemed to stare directly and deeply into Willie's eyes as if he were purposely singling him out, beckoning him.

Willie leaned forward, feeling pulled by some strange force. What an abundance of goodwill and kindness seemed etched on the man's face!

"Friends," the man spoke when the crowd had quieted. "No charge for this fine show you are privileged to witness today. The only price for admission is your undivided attention."

Amid the applause, the man bowed and stepped backward, expertly disappearing between the invisible opening in the folds of the curtain.

Willie kept his eye on the curtain, and before the clapping died away, he saw a dark snout push through the folds and a large, cinnamon-colored bear gallumphed onto the stage. The bear had a leather muzzle strapped over its mouth and a heavy chain fastened to a collar. The trainer, a short man with bulging eyes and a mustache dwarfing his face, carried a whip. Each snap in the air, each flick at the bear's fur, set the animal growling deep in its throat—but then it would obediently rear upright into a lumbering dance.

Willie looked around at the crowd, at Nellie and Jeff, but everyone seemed intent with pleasure at the show. No one seemed to notice the sad eyes of the captive dancing bear.

A spidery monkey in a red hat and jacket came tumbling onstage next. The more the crowd laughed, the wilder the little monkey's antics became. Willie laughed, too, holding onto his sides, forgetting momentarily the misery of the bear.

And then the monocled man stepped forward again. "Ladies and gentleman, for this final act we ask that you remain in your seats. For your own safety, please do not make any sudden movements, and we ask that any small children be removed to the farthest extremities of the show area. You are about to witness the Rattlesnake King as he performs unbelievable feats of control over the devil snake. All the vitrolic vipers you will see today have been captured with little aid other than his bare hands. He has gone into the very den of hell and brought back Satan alive! He has captured and tamed the progenitor of evil in this very land, this very ground you inhabit every day, from along the rocky water-way of the Delaware, and the stony hills where you log the giant hemlocks—this, too, is where the mighty Abraham walks. This, too, is where the deadly timber rattlers thrive. Only one man known to our modern age has no fear of this reptile of Eden. This man is our good friend, the friend of every man, woman, and child. Ladies and gentlemen, I am honored to present Abraham Minckler, the Rattlesnake King Extraordinaire!"

Finally, when Willie felt he could contain himself no longer, the curtains parted—and the tallest man he had ever seen was standing center stage. The man wore clothes like an ordinary woodsman and carried a gunnysack in one hand, through which Willie could see the writhing movement of snakes. This was the mighty Rattlesnake King!

CHAPTER 9

Willie could not take his eyes away from the man before him. Abe stood tall and strong, with feet spread wide and muscles bulging through his shirtsleeves—a real Goliath on a puppet stage. Even the brightness of the day seemed to bow down and with the sun behind him, Abe cast a shadow that stretched across the stage onto Willie.

Abe looked out over the crowd, his gaze settling from time to time on someone's face, and all the while Willie watched him closely and wanted to call out, "Look here! Look at me!" Willie's body wriggled like a pup's, and he practically tumbled off the plank in his eagerness to be noticed. Abe *had* to notice him. But he did not.

When Abe lowered his eyes to take in the front row where Willie sat, it was to Thomas that he looked. And to Thomas that he spoke. "You, lad," he said, pointing straight at the boy. "Are you man enough to be my assistant?"

Thomas leaped to his feet, his chest puffing out with pride. "Sir, I am your man."

Willie swallowed against the painful enormity of the unfairness. Abe should have picked him, but the man had passed right over him as if he weren't even there. And now, Willie knew, he would have to suffer the other boy's gloating and boasts the rest of the day.

As Thomas moved swiftly and confidently to the stage, Willie cast silent curses at the boy's back. A part of him even wished Thomas might be bitten by one of the snakes.

But of course, such a thing could never happen, not with Abraham onstage to protect him, and the job Thomas was given was so simple, anyone but a baby could have done it. All Thomas had to do was stand to the rear of the stage and hand Abe a prop when he called for it.

Scornfully, Willie consoled himself with these thoughts, but his anger faded as quickly as it had come when Abe opened the sack of serpents and tipped it up like a pitcher letting the contents pour out at his feet.

A gasp rippled through the crowd. Dorrie drew close to him again and clutched at his arm; her friends screamed. Willie glanced quickly at Thomas, who stood at the rear of the platform and smiled as if he did this sort of thing every day. Calmly, the boy moved forward and handed Abe a snake pole.

Without haste, Abe took the pole with a metal hook on the end and lightly prodded the snakes, forcing them to glide like fishes swimming in a school.

Willie remained tense, edging forward on the seat.

"They're copperheads, Will-lee," Dorrie whispered in his ear. "They don't have rattles. See how shiny the heads are? Thomas killed one in the school yard once."

This news came as no surprise to Willie. The other boy had probably been hailed as a hero for saving the lives of all the little children. Willie sighed. It was one more thing Thomas was likely to add to his boasts after the show.

Willie's head snapped back in surprise and chills went down his back as Abe took up one of the snakes and spoke: "The Lord said to Moses, 'What is in thine hand?' And Moses replied, 'A rod.'" As Abe said this, the snake went limp in his hands as if it had no will of its own. "And God said, 'Cast it on the ground,' and Moses cast it on the ground and it became a serpent."

Then Abe threw the snake down, and immediately it tried to slither away, but he caught it by the tail and lifted it up, and again, the copperhead went limp as if it were dead.

It was like nothing Willie had ever witnessed. He himself had picked up a garter snake that was sunning itself on the well stone, lifted it up by the tail and dropped it as it twitched furiously, curling its head, flicking its tongue wildly, hissing and opening its mouth. But that was just a garter!

Abe returned all the snakes to their sack and exchanged the first sack for another that was alongside his chair. At once this bag came alive with buzzing and motion. Abe held the bag aloft, shaking it violently. Then he let it fall, quickly motioning for Thomas.

Thomas didn't come forward so boldly this time, Willie noticed with great satisfaction. The boy's face was white, and he stepped back quickly after giving Abe the pole.

Cautiously, Abe loosened the twine with the pole hook. Willie could sense a change in the air all around him, the stillness of a body of people holding their breath as one.

And then the nose of a large rattlesnake appeared. Its head was wide and flat and shaped like a triangle; its neck was slender and as delicate as a young woman's. The head and neck were a yellowish color with dark mottled spots, like fallen leaves on the forest floor.

The snake began to slither from the bag, cautious, its tongue flicking in and out demonically. From time to time, its head jerked back as if it were intending to strike; or it would rear up, its long neck arched, and cast long, unblinking stares over the crowd. The snake continued to move out of its dark prison until at last the tail, entirely black, appeared with a long end of rattles, at least a baby's finger in length. The snake was nearly as long as Abe was tall, and it was close, not more than ten feet away from where Willie was sitting.

Willie looked sharply at Abe. He appeared almost as if he were in a trance, as if the audience were not there, as if in the whole world there were only Abraham and the devil snake.

Abe prodded the giant snake so that it reared up and buzzed its rattles angrily. He prodded again, and the rattler lunged, striking—striking as Abe continued attacking with the hook. The snake struck at its enemy, hissing, its mouth going wide, fangs glinting, gnashing on air. The prey remained invisible, nothing the serpent could grab hold of.

A fly buzzed near Willie's head, lit on his face, and crept across his cheek to his lips. But he could only twitch, he was too afraid to move his arm to brush it away.

Then suddenly the snake seemed to lose interest and attempted to flee instead, streaking in a sudden, swift movement toward the edge of the stage.

A knot of fear coiled itself around Willie, holding him fast. He grasped the plank seat tightly, afraid that he might swoon with fear like some sissy as the snake seemed about to drop over the side.

Deftly, Abe swooped up the devious reptile with his snake hook, and it hung powerless. Abe dropped the snake back into his gunnysack.

Then it was over. The audience seemed to let out a collective sigh of relief. And then came the applause, and more applause, as Abe drew his assistant forward, and Thomas bowed grandly before the cheering crowd. The girls next to Willie clapped and cheered loudly. Willie clapped and cheered along with them, even though he felt the applause should have been for him, but by some strange misfortune, it was not. First Jeff, then Isaac, and now Abe had decided that he was a young stalk not quite able to do a man's work. Somehow, he had to prove them wrong.

CHAPTER 10

As Dr. Granger leapt onto the stage, the treetops began suddenly to rustle, and a light, pleasant wind moved across the flats. In each of his hands the man carried a green-tinted bottle filled with liquid. His feet had barely touched the wooden platform when he began to speak: "Now this tonic has been used by suffering mankind from coast to coast and back again. It's a true, tried remedy. This afternoon it will be sold for the low, low price of a half-dollar a bottle.

"I don't want you to think I'm braggadocious, or egotistical, but I know a man who died from a pain in his head. He died at eleven o'clock at night cursing God. Why? Because he didn't have this tonic. With this tonic that man would have been alive today. With it you'll sleep better, eat better, smoke better, drink better, and be better. You'll say, 'I'm doggone glad I bought that!'"

"I'll take two bottles of that juice, Doc," a man called from the audience.

Willie stood up and edged forward. The coins in

his pocket burned into his skin. Why, it would be like getting eternal life to buy one of those bottles! Judging by the way the men were hollering and waving dollars in the air, the claims of Dr. Granger must be true.

There was a moment when Dr. Granger paused to wipe his brow, and Willie's heart leapt up as the man leaned down and smiled at him. Him! There was no mistake about it. And then he winked. At him! Winked as if the two of them shared some private secret.

Willie took his seat. He felt suddenly calm, assured in some way by Dr. Granger's wink, and he looked on, finally able to enjoy himself for the first time that day.

After a brisk sale in which Willie saw three crates of magic elixir disappear, Dr. Granger came forward again. This time he removed his vest and rolled up his shirtsleeves. He held up a bar of soap. "Cleanliness is next to godliness. You have read it for yourself in the Good Book, you have heard it proclaimed from the pulpit. Now witness for yourselves how my magic peppermint soap will make you as white as snow. Bear witness, good folk." He placed a few drops of water from a vial onto the bar of soap.

The doctor began to lather the bar in his hands, and great suds formed—the likes of which Willie had never seen. Piles of lather dropped onto the platform, and Willie could hear the *oohing* and *ahhing* of the women in the crowd.

"Would a volunteer from among you have courage to come forward and prove my dictum?" The doctor paused and looked out over the audience. "No one? Not one would come forward to be made as white as snow?"

Willie figured no one would come forward, because everyone there, himself included, was scrubbed just about as clean as they would ever get.

Dr. Granger's face bore a most sorrowful expression. "'Though your sins be as scarlet, they shall be made white as snow.' Will no one come forward to be cleansed?"

"Doctor Granger, I will!" A young woman in the back stood up. "I will!" she said, coming forward. "I will be made clean!"

Willie studied the girl as she came near to where he was seated. She was about Nellie's age, he guessed. Her dress was worn and patched, her burnished hair thick and wild and uncaptured by combs or ribbons. She wore no shoes, her face was darkened by the sun as if it had never seen shade or shadow. He had never seen such a creature, and he pondered from where she might have come.

"Could I try it on me feet?" she called as she made her way to the platform. "Me mum says there ain't nothing can get these hoofs clean."

Willie and everyone else laughed. A man somewhere behind him whispered loudly, "Wouldn't hurt her to try that soap elsewhere neither." There were appreciative chuckles all around. If the girl heard, she didn't let on. She strode brashly onstage and flung the wild mane of her hair off her shoulders.

"What's your name, ma'am?" Dr. Granger asked.

"Blanche," she said.

"Blanche, I want you to step right over here. Sit on this chair." He swept up a chair and moved it closer to the platform's edge.

As he talked, the two jugglers appeared again, each with a pail of water.

Blanche sat on the chair, hoisted up her skirts, and plopped one foot into the pail. Willie's heart pounded when he caught sight of her inner thigh. Gaw, it was gorgeous. He'd never seen a woman's leg before.

Immediately, Blanche gave herself over to scrubbing with the magic soap, and the scent of fresh peppermint reached his nose. It was something to see the miraculous transformation as the white lather grew brown and pink flesh appeared. How sweet was her voice as she sang a hymn of praise to God. But Willie couldn't take his eyes off her elevated skirt, waiting for the moment when she lifted her foot from the bucket.

"Lookee here," she said cheerfully, holding up first one and then another of her feet and ankles, more carefully this time so that only her knees showed. "I'm as white as snow."

Guffaws came from several of the men, and a certain disdainful sniffing from the women. Willie saw a strange look flicker across Blanche's face for an instant and her jaw freeze hard, but then she grinned crookedly. "Me maw would be pleased to have a cake, but I've no coin," she said.

Dr. Granger stepped up to her, placed a hand on her thin shoulders. "Blanche, child, because you came forward and proved to the good folk here the miracle of this soap, I make you a gift of this cake and an additional unblemished one for your ma."

Willie stirred in his seat, an emotion surged in his chest like he had never felt before. What a great man! What a grand deed!

"Now for the rest of you fine folk, I am offering my limited stock of this potent magic for one single ten-cent piece for two cakes. That's two bars of godliness for a mere coin."

This time, Willie noticed, the women were uncontrollable in their zeal to get the bars from the jugglers. He could hear the clinking as the coins were tossed into Dr. Granger's box, and the man's words resounded in his ears—"Two bars of godliness for a mere coin."

CHAPTER 11

From the beginning, when Willie had decided to run away, he had looked for signs—looked for them, but only half-believed they were real. What happened next went through him like a lightning bolt and nearly knocked the breath right out of him. He became a believer in signs forever after.

The crowd was shifting away in all directions by this time, except for Willie. Willie stayed, moving only to the spot right in front of Dr. Granger, waiting patiently to be noticed. Even Dorrie had wearied of waiting and abandoned him for her girlfriends.

At last, Dr. Granger looked up from counting his coins. "You, lad, by what name do they call you?" he asked, tilting his head so the sun didn't glare off his monocle.

"Willie, sir. Willie Bishop."

"I noticed you there in the front row. I like the look of you, Will, like the look in your eye. You got dreams of adventure, don't you, Will?"

This time Willie's voice fled, and he could only nod.

Dr. Granger squinted up at the sun and spoke slowly, "You know, Will, the show's fixing to pack up and leave, oh, a wee bit before daylight. I could use a lad like yourself. Course, I would never want a body to come along unless it were as firmly fixed in his mind as the Ten Commandments on a tablet of stone."

Willie could scarcely believe what he was hearing, but along with his voice, his reason seemed to have left him also, and he could not think of one thing to say in the face of this one, this most true sign.

Dr. Granger didn't seem to mind. He gave Willie a broad and welcoming smile. "Better not to speak your mind now. It'll wait." He paused and looked off across the flats to the shaded grove where the box social was being organized, then back to Willie. "Go now and show that sweet young girl of yours a good time." He spoke slowly and nodded to where Dorrie was talking with her friends. "She'll never forget you for it. There's something to be said for a vigilant heart."

With that the doctor grew silent, and Willie, deep in rapturous thought of becoming a part of this great show, walked across the dusty flats to Dorrie.

Tables had been erected in the picnic grove, and one of the tables was covered with a riot of colorfully decorated baskets and boxes. The village undertaker, Mr. Farley, acting as auctioneer, was just asking for the first bid.

Jeff bought Nellie's basket. Certain other baskets, Willie noted, came under furious bidding. The bidders were young men, and the owners of the baskets were genteel-looking girls about Nellie's age.

When Mr. Farley held up Dorrie's basket, Willie fingered the coins in his pocket. It wasn't part of his plan to spend his money. But then Thomas called out, "One half-dollar!"

The coins in Willie's pocket felt even heavier now. He needed—wanted—the money for running away. He swallowed. He just couldn't let Thomas have Dorrie's basket.

"One dollar!" he heard himself say with shock and disbelief. One dollar? It was all the money he had, every cent. He moaned softly with the thought of giving up his precious coins.

It was quiet. Willie held his breath as he watched Thomas searching through his pockets. Then, grinning, he held up a coin. "One dollar ten," Thomas hollered out, looking smugly at Willie.

Thomas had done it, he'd beaten him once again. Defeated, Willie let his arms hang limply at his sides, and when Mr. Farley called out, "Claim your prize, boy!" Willie turned his back and walked away.

CHAPTER 12

Although the sun had not yet set, the hemlock forest was chilly and quite dark when Willie walked Dorrie home. In one hand, Willie swung her empty basket, but when she shivered and edged closer to him, he took her hand into his free one.

"I'm sorry you didn't get my basket at the social," Dorrie said, probably for the hundredth time that afternoon.

"Doesn't matter now," Willie said as his fingers closed more firmly over hers. Dorrie would be hurt if she knew he was running away, and she would never understand why. He hated leaving her this way, but he felt he had no choice.

They walked along in the growing dusk, subdued now by the ending of a fine day. "Dorrie, look," he said in a whisper, pointing through a crack in the canopy of branches. "The sun hasn't set and already the stars are coming out—one star at least."

"It *is* a star!" she said with wonder, gazing upward. They were standing so close that Willie could hear her breathing. "It's a sign of some sort, a sign just for us, don't you think?" she asked.

Willie's heart began to pound, and he moved along, drawing her with him. "It might be a sign," he said slowly, wanting to please her. He gave a great sigh of relief as they came around a bend in the path, and light from the setting sun shone through the opening at the forest's end.

When they came out into the warm light of the sunset, Willie stopped. "Dorrie . . . I . . . I . . ." He swallowed.

"What, Will-lee?" she said, peering anxiously into his face. "What is it?"

"You know we'll always be friends, don't you? And you would never forget me, would you, Dorrie? Even if I made other friends?"

"Will-lee," she said, moving toward him. She leaned against him and rested her head on his shoulder. "How could I ever forget my best friend? We are best friends, aren't we?"

Willie groaned inwardly. How could he leave her? He let the basket slip from his fingers and put his arms around her. "Yes, we're best friends," he said huskily.

He dropped his arms to his sides and took a step away from her, back into the shadow of the forest. "I've got to go now, Dorrie. Got to get back for milking." His voice quavered, and his whole body shook.

He turned and hurried down the darkened path. "Got to go, Dorrie," he called, praying she wouldn't call to him or follow. He almost ran then, fleeing from her, but when he got to the bend he gave a fleeting glance over his shoulder.

Dorrie was still standing at the entrance of the forest, golden sun fanning out around her. He drew in a sharp breath at her image, but turned quickly away into the forest and was swallowed up by the darkness.

CHAPTER 13

It was good that Willie had paid close attention to the landmarks leading to the village, because in the early morning mist and darkness the strange forms of trees were deceiving. Once, he stopped short, certain that he'd seen the movement of a dark figure about his own size. But when he got farther along, there was nothing, no tree, no fence post or shrub. It could, perhaps, have been a bear or deer. Or maybe it had only been a trick of light or the result of his sleepless hours of anxious waiting and excitement. Willie pushed on even faster then. The village was a fair distance—about three hours on foot—but luckily the trip was down the mountain the whole way.

He arrived at the flats in Equinunk with the first hint of light and was relieved to find the bright colors of the show wagons gleaming through the mist. The wagons were lined up and ready to depart. Willie could easily overtake them before they got to the outskirts of the village, and he started to run, calling out as he came upon them.

"Doctor Granger!" Willie called. "Wait for me." He ran alongside the horses and wagons just beginning to move out.

"Come here, boy." The doctor's voice boomed out above the creaking of the wagons and clopping of horses. "I'd just about given up on you," he said as Willie reached the wagon.

Dr. Granger was at the head of the procession. He sat up on a high wagon seat and was as neatly and fashionably attired as he had been at the show, with the noticeable absence of his monocle. He leaned down to Willie now and offered him an arm. "Grab hold of me," he cried. "Don't be afeard, boy. I won't let go of you."

Gladly Willie reached up, and as his arm was seized and he was quite nearly snatched onto the seat, the thoughts of Dorrie, Nellie, and Jeff that had crowded his mind on the way disappeared as quickly as the dark shapes of the mist. He had made it. He was free. He was on his way to somewhere at last.

The road they took was cut into the steep side of a mountain, with moss-covered ledges sprouting laurel and hemlock above and the crash of the river rapids below. Willie clung tightly to the edge of the seat, although the narrowness of the passage did not seem to affect the doctor in the least.

In no time at all, Willie quickly discovered that his companion not only enjoyed the sound of his own voice, but took great pleasure in his own magnificent words.

Dr. Granger bit off the end of a substantial cigar and lit it. He puffed contentedly for a minute, leaving the reins go quite slack in his hands, apparently not in as much of a hurry to get somewhere as Willie had hoped.

"Willie boy, there are many possibilities in this world—opportunities the common man does not see or appreciate."

Willie nodded his agreement. These were wise words, and he listened intently.

"The common man dreams of a parcel of land all his own, a house on that land, a wife in the home to take care of him, and children to carry on his meager plot of earth, to till the same soil, to live in the same house after the good Lord has called him to rest. Yes, Willie, that is the way of the common man. But what of the uncommon man, a man like myself, or a boy like you?" he said, thrusting the end of his cigar toward him. "My boy, what is it that you want?" He paused then and looked gravely into Willie's eyes.

Willie didn't falter. He didn't have to think about this. "Adventure," he blurted out. "Excitement, danger, and towns where something is always going on, and. . ." He broke off suddenly, and didn't go on to say that he wanted a chance to be somebody. Instead he said, "And a chance to do something besides farming. I *hate* farming." Willie sat back, quite struck by the truth of his own words.

"Ah," said the doctor, nodding, seemingly, in approval. A secret sort of smile played on the man's lips as he leaned toward Willie. "Every new place is a new possibility for the uncommon man. But now, Willie, the question to be answered is: What do you want from me?"

This seemed to be a test of some sort, and Willie paused a moment, searching in his mind for the words he supposed the doctor wanted to hear. In his own mind, Willie hoped to be apprenticed to the Rattlesnake King, but Willie suspected this answer would not win the affection of a man like Dr. Granger, and so he said in his most winsome way, "Sir, I wish to become your apprentice, but I am willing to accept even the humblest and most menial tasks to be a part of your great show."

The doctor laughed aloud at this reply and slapped Willie quite firmly on the back. "My boy! My boy! You are fashioned out of the same rich fabric as myself. It will be any task for you now. However, if I read your look correctly, you shall become my apprentice someday. Now tell me, what is your expertise—where do your talents lie?"

"What do you mean, exactly, sir?" Willie asked politely. He did not think the doctor should know of his thieving capabilities, an expertise he may have lost since being on the farm for so long.

"I mean, can you sing? Can you play? Can you dance? Can you . . ." But the man broke off, his lips forming unsaid words, his hands stirring the air.

Willie could only guess what it was he had changed his mind about.

"I can sing—a little. I can play the harmonica. Dancing goes quite naturally with those talents, don't you think, sir?" Willie said, being careful not to say that his only experience with dancing had been in the avoidance of being trotted around by a silly girl at Liberty Hall when he and Nellie still lived in Dyberry Forks.

"My, my, but you are a crafty soul. I like that, boy. I do like that. Well, now, play us a melody, son."

Willie did, and as he played he watched the doctor out of the corner of his eyes. Dr. Granger slumped against the seat back and began to take long swallows from a silver flask, and Willie feared mightily that he was displeased and thought the performance poor or else that the man was paying him no heed at all.

Finally, Willie mustered the courage to speak. "Sir," he said, slipping his harmonica back into his pocket. "Can I still be an apprentice?"

Like magic, Dr. Granger swept the flask out of sight and cleared his throat. Without taking his eyes off the dusty road, the man seized Willie's wrist and gripped it tightly. "Boy, you will do. You will do very well," he said, letting go of Willie's arm.

CHAPTER 14

The wagons traveled several miles through the narrow pass before they came out of the shadow of the mountain and the dark forest of hemlock, laurel, and rhododendron. As the morning sun broke through the mist, the surroundings became bathed with yellow light.

There were flowers in bloom along the roadside and an abundance of buttercups and golden paintbrushes in the cow pastures. Swarms of small yellow butterflies danced over the meadows. It was almost as if they had stumbled upon a new land. If only Dorrie could see this, Willie thought. . . .

Remembering Dorrie, Willie felt pained for an instant. But then, thankfully, he was rescued by Dr. Granger's voice swelling up suddenly like a bullfrog's. "Boy," he hollered, straightening his back and slipping his monocle into place. "We're coming to a small hamlet—Stockport. Keep your hat tipped forward, over your face, if you follow me, but keep your back straight, so as to give the impression of importance."

"Will we be stopping, sir?" Willie asked as he arranged his hat to cover his eyes. "Will you do a show here?"

"Do you know any folk from these parts, boy?"

Willie shook his head. He couldn't name one.

"Someone may know you by sight, if not by name. I suppose you are aware of the implications here?" Dr. Granger said, looking askance at Willie.

"I . . . uh . . . I suppose," Willie said. He had been so eager to be identified as one of the troupe that he had already forgotten his own concern of being recognized.

Nevertheless, as they drove through the small settlement, everyone within sight stopped their chores to wave, and a crowd of children flocked to the wagons like young crows to a shiny object. Travel became nearly impossible and quite perilous. Despite the clamoring voices of children begging for entertainment, the doctor forged ahead. He waved in a friendly manner, with a broad smile gleaming from his face—but he did not stop.

Willie was afraid to speak up, but he thought it a little mean of Dr. Granger not to favor the children with even a bit of a show. He slumped against the seat back and sulked. Even after they had passed through the throng and entered a wood again, Willie would not look at his benefactor.

"So soon you are a malcontent, I see? So soon you question my judgment and my motives. You, a lad, who certainly understand the whys and wherefores of show business, no doubt you think me a querulous old man," the doctor said, whisking his cigar from a hidden pocket and relighting it.

Willie could feel his face growing warm with color.

"As I thought," Dr. Granger said with a click of his tongue. "*Tsk. Tsk.* Shall I let you off, boy?"

Willie shook his head violently, but his tongue seemed swollen and useless. He studied the man's face closely now. Did he mean it? Could he possibly?

Dr. Granger laughed. A look of glee came into his eyes, spreading across his face. "Well . . . well . . . so that's how it is. No harm done. You will learn the whys and wherefores soon enough."

CHAPTER 15

They had gone several miles past Stockport. Now the sun was quite high, and its earlier charm was gone. In the heat, the leaves and flowers drooped wearily. Willie was relieved when the wagons pulled off the road and drove over to a stand of trees beside the river. There was an open meadow nearby, and the air was cooler. Dr. Granger brought the wagon to a halt beneath an ancient beech.

Willie jumped down from the wagon seat. He was eager to put his hand to any type of work the doctor might find for him, but he was even more eager to be with the rest of the troupe—and Abe in particular.

"Ah, the perfect location," Dr. Granger said, running his eyes across the landscape. "Come with me, my boy."

They didn't go far, only to the door of the wagon. The doctor rapped. "Daughter, open up," he called.

The door swung open, and there stood a girl about Nellie's age. She was dressed like a boy—in overalls and checkered shirt—and her chestnut hair was braided and wrapped in tight coils around her head. From a distance, she could easily be mistaken for a boy. There was a deep frown on her face.

It took a moment before Willie realized who the girl was, and then his stomach did a curious flip. It was Blanche— the wild girl onstage at the show in Equinunk!

"Da-daughter," Willie spluttered looking from the girl to Dr. Granger. "Bla-Blanche is your daughter?"

The silver-haired man laughed and patted Willie's head. "You're learning the whys and where-fores, boy. It's all part of the show game, son," the doctor said with a wink as he ushered him into the heart of the wagon.

It was like a little house, really, with sleeping berths, a crudely made stove, cupboards, a kerosene lamp, pots and pans, a shelf of books, a green velvet chair with an ornately carved wooden back, a window with red calico curtains. The place had a compact tidiness that reminded Willie of his brother-in-law, although Willie felt sure no two people could be more different than Dr. Granger and Jeff.

With the air of a ruling monarch, the doctor seated himself in the chair and relit his cigar. "So, daughter, this is your new apprentice, the boy I told you about—Willie Bishop."

Willie bristled. Apprentice? To a girl! Was this what the man meant by any task? "What about the show? Can't I be in the show? Sir, you said . . ." he blurted out.

Dr. Granger raised his eyebrows and puffed a

cloud of smoke in Willie's direction. "Patience, young man," he said in his usual benevolent manner, "all things in good time."

Still, Willie bent his head and swallowed hard against this unexpected blow. He felt cruelly tricked.

"I told you, I don't need anyone. I don't want anyone," Blanche said fiercely. "I'm fine by myself—alone," she said, moving to the doorway.

A gray shadow seemed to cross the doctor's face. "Today, maybe . . . in daylight," he said, his voice suddenly grave.

Blanche swung around. "How can you be so certain that this runaway will be any different from all the others?"

Willie glanced wildly from Blanche to her father. Other runaways? When? What did Blanche mean?

"Trust me on this one," Dr. Granger said, pointing his cigar in Willie's direction.

Blanche narrowed her eyes. "We'll just see about that!"

The man shook his head. "No further discourse, child, I have to deliberate and pontificate my new pitch," he said, waving his hand in a dismissive way. "Take the kid with you, and don't let him out of your sight."

"Whatever you say, Your Highness," Blanche said. "Come on, kid," she said, stepping down out of the wagon. "We've got work to do."

Kid. He was nothing but a kid to the doctor, not an

uncommon boy of many possibilities. Stunned by the demeaning words, Willie moved with heavy feet down the steps of the caravan behind Blanche. For now he would play this game by the rules, but he'd be alert for possibilities. Even now, he looked around him for signs of Abe. Though he could hear voices, everyone seemed mysteriously hidden from his sight.

"Where is everyone?" Willie asked, watching as Blanche unstrapped a huge iron pot from the back of the wagon.

"Everyone here works. Everyone. Everyone does exactly what Doc says."

"Even the Rattlesnake King?"

"Oh, you mean, Abe?" she said. She shook her head. "He's part of the show, but he's not with us, exactly. He follows the show in the summer. In the autumn he goes back home, to log, or raft or something."

"Then, he's only around for the shows?"

"Sort of. You'll see," she said. "Now grab the other handle."

Willie took hold of the kettle. How would he ever get to know Abe if Abe came and went like a ghost? How could he ever hope to become Abe's apprentice? Aloud he asked, "What the heck do you do with a kettle this big?"

"Cauldron," Blanche corrected as they carried the iron pot toward the river. "I make Doctor Granger's Ginger Beer—the magic elixir with miracle curative powers," she said, mimicking her father's show pitch.

"You? You actually make it?" Willie asked suspiciously.

"Me," Blanche said proudly. "I'm the only one who knows how."

"You're going to teach me to make potion?" Willie asked, suddenly interested in this new occupation.

"Not potion . . . medicine, good medicine, medicine that cures. And I'm not a quack, I know what I'm doing," Blanche said fiercely. "Mum used to make the medicine, and I helped her when she was alive. When Mum was alive, the show wasn't a . . . a tramp show. We were a real show almost as big as the Kickapoo Indian Show or Hamlin's Wizard. We didn't have buffalo dances and rifle shootings but we had razzle-dazzle and as a good a ballyhoo as any show, and a real band riding into town on a wagon. We put on plays—folks came back every night for more than a week. Every night we had crowds to see the same show, and I got to be in the show. I was the little girl who died in the end. The women cried, sometimes the men, too. We went back to the same towns every year, and the farmers and the townfolk loved us. They really loved us. And then everything changed. Now all we have are old, broken-down men, mangy, flea-bitten animals, or runaway rubes from the sticks who don't know better. Doc blames our hard times on the Kickapoo shows, but it's not them. We'd still be a big show if Mum hadn't died."

Blanche stopped when they got to the river's edge, and Willie helped her set up the kettle on some worn, rounded stones. He didn't like to mention that she had not even come close to answering his question, and he hadn't a notion of how to bring it up after her amazing speech. "Well . . ." he said, searching for a way to begin.

"Well, stop gawking at me," Blanche said, wide-eyed. "Go on, gather up all the driftwood you can for a fire."

CHAPTER 16

Willie seethed as he gathered driftwood along the shoreline. Wasn't it just his kind of luck to get tangled up with a broken-down tramp show? This very minute he could be having a great adventure in a Kickapoo show—rifle shootings, buffalo dances, bands, plays . . . But no, he had to run off and hook up with low-down, lying Doc, his mean-mouthed, bratty daughter, and their mangy old show.

At that moment, Willie heard the long, lonely whistle of a train in the distance. It was a good ways off, but it was as if his ear had been tuned to this sound above all. He hurried to add his wood to the fire before the train came into view. He saw the plume of smoke rising above the tops of the trees on the opposite shore and then the train itself burst into view as if fired from a cannon. Willie felt its movement through his chest, and his heart beat in time to the *clickety-clackety clack* and squeal of the wheels. "Gawd, ain't that the purtiest sight," he said dreamily.

He jumped when Blanche spoke. "I think it's powerful mean-looking," she said.

Willie stared as the train disappeared with smoke and sparks of fire trailing across its back, and then the day was quiet again. Too quiet.

"Blanche," he said slowly. "What did Doc mean when he said I was different from the other runaways?"

"*He* said that, not me," she said scowling. "Runaways, like you, don't stay with the show long—but *you* will. That's what Doc meant, I think," she said, biting her lip and turning her face away.

She wasn't telling him everything, Willie was certain. He studied her profile, but it gave away nothing.

"So why did you do it?" she asked, turning back to give him a hard stare.

"Do what?"

"Run away."

"I wanted to be in the show with Abe, and Doc acted as if I would be. I wanted to go places, be in towns, and . . ." Willie shrugged.

"And what?" Blanche asked, watching his eyes.

Willie's shoulders slumped. "And nothing," he said in a sorrowful voice.

"Listen," she said, her voice gentle for the first time. "Abe's probably on that train we just saw. We'll meet him tonight or tomorrow in Hancock for the next show."

"Abe rides the rails?" Willie asked hopefully.

Blanche nodded. "Or goes on foot," she said. "But

come on now, we've got to gather the herbs."

Willie followed her into the woods, some distance from the caravans. He was puzzled by the sudden change in her.

"You're not a thief, are you, Willie?" she asked, suddenly, stopping by a fallen, decaying tree covered with moss and plants.

Willie could feel the color rush into his cheeks, but he shook his head.

"More's the pity." She sighed, and bent over to pull up a plant by the roots. She held out the plant to him. "Ginseng," she said. "Study it closely, know the exact leaf formation, the look of the roots, the location of the flower on the stem, the color and number of petals on the blossom. But beware! One imposter in the bunch will poison the whole brew."

Willie looked at her with new respect. This was no trick. She was teaching him real stuff.

"Pick all of them through here," she said, waving her arm in a circle around her.

Willie squatted down and examined each plant before pulling one up and adding it to Blanche's pile.

"Can you read?" Blanche asked sharply.

Willie blinked in surprise. "Of course I can. Who can't?" he scoffed, although he could name a number himself.

"Good," she said, moving away from him toward the open meadow.

He trailed along.

"Doc will want you to read the books on his shelf, and the Bible, too. The Bible mostly . . . I think." She stopped suddenly. "Bergamot," she said, bending over. She broke the stem of a purple flowering plant that had bees and butterflies swarming over it.

"Have you read the books? Are they any good?" he asked, rapidly pulling up handfuls of the plant. The crushed leaves were sweet-smelling, like honey.

Blanche held a flower to her nose, and then nibbled on a leaf. It was several moments before she answered, and she moved away from him as she spoke. "No . . . not yet. Someday. I have so much to do for the mighty Doctor Granger," she said bitterly. "Do you like books, though?"

"Not much, not dreary schoolbooks, not clocution with vocal expression and principles of action," Willie said in a prim mocking fashion.

"Could you tell me more about this . . . el-o-cu-tion?" Blanche asked.

"Sure, sure, it's sort of like what Doc does," Willie said.

"Doc's pitch has a fancy name like that?" Blanche asked.

Willie dropped his armful of wild bergamot. "Sit down and be a proper audience. I'll show you how we're made to do it in school."

Blanche seated herself in the meadow grass, her arms still laden with sweet flowers.

Willie cleared his throat and began:

"The Barefoot Boy
by John Greenleaf Whittier.
Blessings on thee, little man,
Barefoot boy, with cheek of tan!"

Willie threw his arms out stiffly in all directions and made his voice rise up and down in a jerky way. Blanche began to laugh, her face bright with pleasure. Encouraged by this, Willie continued:

"With thy turned-up pantaloons,
And thy merry whistled tunes;
. . . Outward sunshine, inward joy:
Blessings on thee, barefoot boy!"

Willie bowed low and then dropped, laughing, in the grass next to Blanche.

Blanche clapped. "Willie, you were so comical," she said, her voice full of gentle laughter. "Will you do it again for me sometime?"

"At your service, ma'am," Willie said, bobbing his head and feeling pleased. "But wait till we get to town. Newspapers are what I like. They have the best stories, Blanche. Western serials, stories of Indians and real adventure . . ."

He caught a sly look flash in her eyes, and her mouth twisted with a mysterious smile. "I would like it if you read to me when I'm working. Would you like that, Willie?" she asked. "We can get you newspapers in every town we go through."

Willie nodded. "I'd like that very much," he said as they set to work again gathering more plants. The girl puzzled him mightily. Her moods reminded him of a seesaw. He crushed a stem of the sweet bergamot in one hand and glanced over at Blanche, absorbed in her work. Was Blanche being nice to him because she wanted something? What could Blanche possibly want from him?

CHAPTER 17

Willie stood by respectfully and watched as Blanche added small bunches of the herbs they had gathered to the simmering pot, stirring them with a sturdy stick.

Finally, she turned to him. "Stir this for me, Willie, until the sun is there and your shadow falls beside you here," she said pointing to the sky and ground. "I have to get dried ginger root from the caravan."

Willie looked at the sky and then down at his shriveled-up shadow. He sighed. He would be stuck with this cauldron for a good long time, and who knew what great things were going on at the caravans? They might be practicing for the show or telling stories about their adventures, and he was missing it all. The cauldron was hot; the iron pot shimmered with radiant heat. The sun bore down.

"I'll go," Willie said in an offhanded way, as if the errand held no real interest for him.

Blanche backed away from him with a wounded look in her eyes, which was quickly replaced by a scowl.

"You think this is just some game, don't you?"

"Doc said . . . ." Willie's voice trailed off into silence, and he did what he always did in moments of uncertainty—he shrugged.

"Just go, go on, go back to the troupe. That's what you want, isn't it, to be with the men, the real performers?"

Willie nodded slowly. "Can I, Blanche?" he asked, already moving away.

"You can go back where you came from, for all I care, Willie Bishop," she said. Turning away from him, she began to stir the elixir again.

Willie fairly stumbled over the rocks and scrambled up the sloping bank. Then he went through the woods toward the caravans. His stomach was grumbling in hunger. He'd had just a hunk of bread that morning, saved over from supper the night before, and already the sun was past high noon.

Before he came into the clearing, he could smell beans and pork and hear the voices of men cheering, with an occasional whistle or clap of hands.

He rushed toward the old beech, and was just about to call out an excited "Hallo" when he stopped short. He took a cautious step backward, then another, and then he hid himself behind a nearby tree. His heart thumped loudly, and a fist of pain exploded in his chest. It seemed Doc and all the performers but Abe were there, but that wasn't the problem. The problem was a juggler—a boy tossing balls—in the midst of them all.

This new juggler was not a boy, exactly. Willie figured he was seventeen, maybe even as old as eighteen, but not as old as Jeff—who was in his twenties. He was sporting a mustache like everyone else old enough to grow one, Willie noted ruefully as he fingered his own smooth chin. The young man was solidly built, his bare chest and arms rippling with muscles, and though he was not a giant like Abe, he was taller than the other men in the troupe.

Willie remained motionless, hardly breathing. He watched the handsome youth beneath the limbs of the beech tree nimbly tossing the balls up among the branches, over the branches, and twirling around to catch them behind his back. Occasionally he added a handspring or some other sort of acrobatic contortion.

Every eye was on the other boy—even the poor bear chained to a tree watched—and the monkey, who sat on the shoulder of its trainer, chattered and clapped its little hands at the young man's tricks. Worst of all was Doc smiling, clapping, and cheering with gusto between puffs on his cigar and drinks from his silver flask. Doc had not clapped or cheered for Willie, and it seemed that a sweet air of jocularity and camaraderie had enclosed the group in an invisible circle—from which he was shut out. Willie hoped the young man would clumsily drop the balls, or stumble over a ground root—but he did not. No doubt this boy would perform onstage in the next town, while he, Willie the dunce, gathered stupid weeds for a girl.

Willie turned away from the scene in the clearing, slumping to the ground at the foot of the tree. His face burned with shame and anger. Who was this boy? Where had he come from? Was he a runaway like himself? Why hadn't he performed in Equinunk?

Willie fished the knife from his pocket and sliced it through a fallen branch stem. For a moment a wave of homesickness shuddered through his body. He thought of Dorric, of Nellie and Jeff, and he longed to be back with them.

But he couldn't go back, he decided as he whittled away bark and chips of wood from the stick. Going back would be a worse shame even than this. He had come too far, and whatever misadventure claimed him, he would keep going.

The whittling calmed him somehow, and he became conscious once again of his surroundings, although how much time had passed he couldn't say. He heard the sounds of the performers practicing in the beech woods, but he had no desire to watch anymore. Instead, he stared toward the river.

Below, through an opening in the trees he could see Blanche sitting alone on a large rock near the iron pot. There was something very sad about the way her head was bent. Why did she stay off by herself? Why didn't she join in with the others?

Without looking back, Willie got quietly to his feet and put his pocketknife away. Moving as silently as he could, he hiked back down to where she was sitting. Where else could he go?

When he was quite near, he called softly, "Blanche?"

She whirled around to face him. "Why did you come back?" she snapped.

Willie shrugged. "Everybody was working," he lied. "Figured I might as well come back and help you." He walked toward the cauldron.

Blanche slid off the rock and stood up next to him and looked him in the eyes. "You're lying," she said.

Willie nodded, his shoulders slumping, and he looked down at the ground. "I saw the other boy, and everyone was watching him."

"Oh, I see," Blanche said. She paused. "That's Adam. He joined up with us about a week ago. I don't recall just where."

"He was juggling and he's . . . he's . . . "

"Doc says he's a magnificent, world-class talent," Blanche said.

"I guess *he's* going to be the new star performer."

"I guess," Blanche said, gently this time.

"I guess you'd rather have him as your apprentice," Willie said, recalling the handsome looks of the older boy.

Blanche gave Willie a stony look. "I guess you'd have no inkling about what I want," she said roughly, squinting up at the sun. "Come on, back to work," she said. "We've crates and crates of little green bottles to fill with Doctor Granger's Magic Elixir before the sun hits the tree line. I already went for the ginger root myself."

They went back to get the crates, and then began

the job of filling the bottles. Willie soon discovered that the generous size of the bottle was much more important-looking than what the inside could hold.

He and Blanche each had a funnel, a supply of corks, and crates of bottles imprinted with Dr. Granger's name. It was a tedious task, ladling the green liquid into the potion bottles, but Willie's mind was taken up with the more serious matter of this Adam who had suddenly appeared. The troupe would soon be getting to Hancock. The possibilities of what Willie might do once in town spun in his mind like a whirligig. His hands fairly shook with impatience to be done with this outfit and move on.

When they had loaded up the wagon and tied the kettle securely in place, Doc sashayed up, smiling and in obvious high spirits. He patted Willie on the back. "My boy," he said. "Did I forget to mention that you'll be riding inside with Blanche from now on?"

"But, sir . . ." Willie swallowed. "I thought . . . I was hoping . . . that is, I wanted . . ."

Doc raised a hand to silence him. "Don't speak rashly, son," he said. "Your concern will be discussed and favorably resolved at a future time." With that, Doc turned and hurried to take his seat up high at the head of the troupe.

"I suppose next I'll be getting a collar and he'll have me tied up like Belle the Dancing Bear Wonder," Willie muttered at Doc's back. He followed Blanche up the steps of the caravan. Just as he was about to go through the doorway, he turned around.

Adam was standing alongside the last caravan. One of the jugglers was holding a costume up to him.

At that moment the older boy glanced over and caught sight of Willie. But Willie shrunk back into the shadows and ducked quickly inside. He was ashamed to be nothing more than Blanche's helper, and he didn't want to be friends with this new boy.

Inside Blanche bustled around the little room, humming as she took a tin of Vermont crackers from a cupboard and set it on the table alongside a chunk of cheddar. The cheese looked as yellow as Willie was feeling inside. Coward, that's what he was.

Blanche interrupted his thoughts. "I suppose you're used to having good meals all the time at home," she said apologetically as she lifted the cover from the tin.

Before Willie could reply, there was a sudden lurch of the wagon, and they were off.

CHAPTER 18

Willie knew it as soon as they reached the out-skirts of Hancock sometime later—knew it before any sounds reached his ear or buildings could be seen. "Listen," he whispered to Blanche.

Blanche laid her sewing in her lap and tilted her head to one side.

Even above the creaking of their own wagons and the rocking motion that set the furniture and fixtures to jiggling, Willie knew. "It's town, Blanche. We've come upon a town," he said, his skin tingling with excitement.

No sooner had he said this than the sounds burst upon his ears—hammers pounding wood, the clanging sound of a smithy, and the echoing reports.

Without a word, Blanche moved to the window and pinned back the curtains. He crowded next to her to look.

Willie grasped the edge of the open window and pushed his face out to breathe in the town air. His eyes roamed over every detail—every sign and building they passed, every person and buggy going by on the dusty street. He drank it all in as if he had worked all day in the sun and had finally come to drink from a deep, cool well.

"Blanche!" he cried, grabbing her wrist. "Look at that." Right on the very street they were traveling was a row of hotels, one after another, each with proud wooden faces and high-pillared porches. They seemed enormous in height and stature, with hundreds of glass eyes winking at him in the sunlight.

"It's better than . . . than—" The procession came to a sudden halt in front of the largest hotel, and Adam and the two jugglers darted across the street to the boardwalk in front of the buildings. They began to juggle balls among themselves so skillfully that it was like watching some sort of magic act.

At once a crowd began to gather—people wandering out of open doors, buggies tying up to the rail, children running from all directions. After a few minutes, Adam began passing out handbills and calling out, "Free show, ma'am. Free show, sir." His face glowed like an angel's in the Methodist Illustrated Bible. The group of onlookers seemed noticeably drawn to the boy's agreeable manners.

Willie grasped the window ledge. "Why Adam? Why not me? What's wrong with me?" he blurted out.

Blanche gave him a sisterly pat. "Now, Willie, he *is* older, and stronger, and he can juggle."

Willie shook off Blanche's hand. "That's no reason," he muttered.

Blanche laughed. "You'd do better to fancy the moment," she said, pointing toward the open doorway of one of the hotels.

Out of the shadows of the American Hotel came a giant of a man. It was Abe, the Rattlesnake King! In one hand he carried a gunnysack writhing with motion. There were gasps from the crowd and a ripple of screams among the womenfolk as they fell back to let him pass. Willie forgot his earlier troubles.

"Oh, Blanche," he said with a moan. "Mightn't I go out there?"

Blanche laid a restraining hand on his arm and shook her head. "Not yet, Willie. You'll get your chance."

To a brave few, Abe opened his sack, but after just a glance, the people flinched and stepped away.

"I'll bet I could do that. I'll bet I could even hold that old sack, if I had even half a chance," Willie muttered.

Blanche had an amused look on her face. "Could you now?" she asked, the corners of her mouth twitching. "Suppose one of those big rattlers got riled up and struck out at you?" she said, grabbing at him, her hands fashioned like open jaws, sinking into his arm like fangs.

Willie jumped back and uttered a cry of alarm.

Blanche laughed aloud. "See what I mean," she said smugly, crossing her arms over her waist.

"I could do it, I know I could," he muttered, looking back out the window. In just those few seconds, Abe had disappeared and the jugglers were crossing back to the caravans. Willie was about to duck out of sight when Adam, no more than six yards away, looked straight at the window and raised a hand in greeting. Willie froze, his body swept over with the heat of feeling caught. But this time he managed a feeble wave before backing away from the window.

CHAPTER 19

The wagons began moving again. Willie noticed that the wind had picked up, and loose dirt was scuffling and swirling along the wheel-rutted street. The western sun, which had burned so brazenly all day, had now disappeared behind a curtain of clouds.

The little troupe of wagons continued down the main thoroughfare, and Adam and the other two jugglers ran ahead at times to tack up handbills. All through the town, the procession was greeted by cheers of children leaving their games to run alongside—shopkeepers in aprons coming out of their stores, businessmen in suits pausing to stare. The welcoming, congenial looks and hand-waving stirred a powerful excitement in Willie, and he longed to holler, to burst out of his prison and run along with the other children. It no longer seemed to matter that the show was small or that Adam got to pass out the handbills, because here the troupe seemed as welcome as a sudden rain in an August drought.

In his mind, Willie pictured the distingushed Doc, sitting up on the high seat in front, his monocle securely in place as he waved to the admiring crowd. Willie thought how grand he himself would look up there beside Doc—if only he were given a chance.

The wagons continued to the far end of town until they reached a floodplain washed over by cobblestones and silt. Tufts of weeds and rushes grew here and there. The caravans halted close to the river and the railroad tracks beneath a cluster of tall poplars.

In a moment, there was a knock on the door of the caravan, but Blanche stayed at the window, staring out.

"I'll get it," Willie offered, dashing to the door and lifting the inside latch. "Hallo," he cried as he swung open the door and Doc's face appeared. The man climbed up the steps and entered the room. Quickly, Blanche turned away from the window and picked up the costume she was mending.

Scowling, Doc strode over and peered outside. "What was of such great interest to you outside until I came in?" he asked, frowning down at his daughter.

"Nothing, Doc," Blanche said meekly enough, without looking up from her sewing.

Doc studied her bent head for a moment, then, seemingly satisfied with her answer, turned back to Willie. "It's going to be a great crowd, a great show tonight," he said, rubbing his hands together in a washing motion.

Willie drew himself up straight, hoping he'd

appear taller to Doc. "I'm honored to be one of your performers, sir," he said.

Dr. Granger laughed. "Now I haven't forgotten you, boy," he said, placing a hand on Willie's shoulder. "You will be a part of the new revival of this once great show. You'll do more than just play that little harmonica of yours. You'll dance, sing, perform in plays. Now, I've been giving it considerable thought the whole time since you signed on, considerable thought, son. But, you understand, one doesn't become a big star overnight, nor a big show overnight. It takes genius, genuine effort, and grand design." Doc leaned toward Willie, squinting one eye as if he were trying to hold the absent monocle in place. Willie caught the distinct smell of whiskey on the man's breath and wondered if Doc would even be fit to do the show that night.

"But . . . but . . ." Willie spluttered, sliding his eyes toward Blanche in the hope of her support. But although Blanche still held the garment, with her needle in mid-stitch, her face was turned again to the open window.

Doc held up a cautioning hand. "Patience, one of God's own virtues, must be exercised."

"Please let me do something!" Willie blurted out, unable to control his impatience another second.

"Why, son, you've been of good service already. However, God does despise idle hands," Doc said, leaving Willie to wonder if the man meant his own self or the God of heaven.

"Go on out to Ivan, the little trainer, and help set up the show." At that, Doc grabbed up several of the new bottles of medicine and slipped them into a deep pocket on the inside of his coat.

Willie stood rooted to the spot. Ivan? He couldn't mean the cruel little man with the whip?

"Well, go on," Doc said brusquely, and then seemed to remember his generous nature once again. "Don't forget, boy, that I'm working out the new show and you will be in it," he said. "But go on with you now." Doc waved his hand as if brushing away a fly, and there was nothing else for Willie to do but go.

CHAPTER 20

Outside the sun had been completely swept away by clouds, and the wind, although meek enough, whispered threateningly in the treetops.

Willie slouched toward the mean-faced animal trainer with only the meager consolation that he did not have to work side by side with Adam the Great.

Already, the horses had been unharnessed and were grazing in the small patches of grass beneath the trees. The less fortunate bear was tied to one of the wagons, and the monkey roamed freely over the bear's massive body searching out vermin.

Adam and the jugglers were busily engaged in setting up the stage in front of their caravan, and just as Willie reached Ivan the trainer, Doc rode past them on his way back toward town. Willie watched as he disappeared on his horse in a cloud of dust. Oh, if only he might be with him . . . if only he might be in town this very moment.

Ivan grunted, and Willie reluctantly tore his gaze away from the horizon and turned toward him. With the fingers of one hand, the man curled the ends of his droopy mustache. With his other hand he made sharp gestures, and he strutted, his head twitching like a rooster about to fight.

Willie tried to do what he thought the man wanted, but at every turn he was pummeled by a stream of harsh oaths. Ivan's ability to cuss would've been splendid if the words weren't directed at Willie's bumbling attempts to secure ropes and drive tent stakes.

Nearby, Willie could hear the friendly exchange of talk and occasional laughter between Adam and the jugglers. When the peals of laughter rang out, he believed it must be directed at him, at his awkward blunders. A fiery heat shot through his body, but it had little to do with the effort from work.

"Aw right, aw right," Ivan said gruffly, shaking his head. "You do mighty fine."

Willie looked up from his labor with surprise. "Me?" he asked.

Ivan grunted. "Ivan give more work."

This time Ivan showed him how to brush the bear. "Brush and brush and brush," Ivan said.

Willie took the brush and pulled it through Belle's fur the way Ivan had done. The bear seemed to like him, or at least like the way he brushed.

The little monkey, Koko, chattered madly at first, but soon settled down on Ivan's shoulder. Ivan nodded and grunted his satisfaction with Willie's work and then disappeared into his own caravan.

"Brush Belle the Bear, brush and brush and brush," Willie said, making it into a little tune.

Willie sang, and Belle swayed, and all was well until he heard a crunching noise behind him. He stopped and turned around.

Adam, his clothes soiled, his face smudged with dirt and streaked with sweat, smiled down at him. "Name's Adam," he said, grabbing Willie's free hand and shaking it. "Adam Johnson."

Willie withdrew his hand and studied the older boy carefully as he said, "I am Willie. . . . Willie Bishop."

"Glad to meet you, finally," Adam said, giving him a friendly slap on the back. "So what made you hook up with Doctor Granger?"

Willie shrugged. "Don't like farming much," he said lamely, not wanting to give away too much.

Adam laughed in such a good-natured way that Willie found himself laughing, too.

"Same here," Adam said. "I'll tell you one thing, Willie, I sure was glad to see another fella younger than creation around here." He wrinkled his forehead. "So what's Doc going to have you do in the show?"

Willie looked at the ground. He should have seen this question coming, and now he was tongue-tied as usual. "Uh . . . uh," he muttered trying to buy some time to think. "Well . . . uh, I play the harmonica. Doc really likes the way I play."

"So what are you playing tonight?" Adam asked.

He was so good-natured and friendly, Willie felt his grudge melting away. "I'm not going to be in the show," he said straight out.

"Why not?" Adam asked, pushing his hat back on his head. He seemed honestly concerned.

"I don't know," Willie said, feeling sick at heart all over again.

"Well, it's my first night performing, and I've been with the show for a week. Probably Doc will have you up onstage for the next show or the next town. I'm sure it won't be long," Adam said kindly.

"You really think so?"

"I wouldn't know why not," Adam said. "But it's darn hard to wait, isn't it, when you've run off hoping to make something of yourself?"

Willie nodded, the older boy's words seemed to soak into him like a healing salve.

"Back to work," Adam said cheerfully. "I'll see you later, after the show," he called as he loped back toward the stage.

Willie watched him go. This Adam was not a bad sort, not like Thomas Thorne at all. In fact, Adam even understood what he was thinking and just how he felt about the show, and for the first time Willie wondered what sort of life this new boy had left behind.

CHAPTER 21

A flurry of activity, the bustle and importance of preparations, swirled around the little show grounds. But for now Willie's work was done, and he was not to be in the show.

Blanche found him at last, her hands filled with strange roots, her face smeared with mud, and he gratefully followed her into the caravan.

"I have to change into costume now," she said gently. She took some twine from a tin on the shelf and tied the roots together and strung them up from a nail in a ceiling beam.

Willie didn't budge. "Blanche," he said. "Let me be in the show. I could sit with you. I could be your poor brother. Please?"

"Oh, Willie," she said, her face getting a tender, doting look so that he thought he had won.

"Please, Blanche, please?" he begged once more.

Blanche shook her head. "Don't look so woebegone," she said. "You will have plenty to do in time, more than you want if the truth is to be known," she said, her voice suddenly weary. "Stand guard outside my door," she said, giving him a gentle push. "I won't take long to dress, I promise. Then you can come back in." She turned away from him and began pouring fresh water into a washbasin. "I'll make it up to you," she said. "Go on with you now."

Willie leaped to the ground without using the steps. Instantly, the door was shut behind him. Seemed as if he was always getting shooed away like he was some pesky old horsefly.

He squatted down next to the caravan and looked around. The little show grounds had become suddenly silent and empty. Everyone, including Adam, must be dressing for the show. He saw Doc's horse tied up with the others, but the man himself was nowhere in sight. No one, he realized with a start, would miss him if he were to slip away, sneak off into town, because they would be too busy with the show. Blanche would discover him missing soon enough, but he somehow didn't think she would raise a hue and cry after him.

He dropped to the ground and crawled on his belly between the axles of the caravan. Moving quietly, he looked cautiously around as if he were an Indian scout. No one was stirring when he poked his head out the far end of the wagon. He got quickly to his feet and fled into the growing dusk as if he were being pursued, hunted down like an escaped horse thief. He did not look back.

Willie hurried down the deserted main street of town, the street they had recently paraded through.

For the first time he was glad that he had not been out on the street. No one here would recognize him nor think he was with the show. He was free.

He walked straight up to the American Hotel, where he had seen Abe earlier, stood on the threshold of the open door, and peered inside. It was hazy with smoke and smelled of cigars, dirty kerosene lamps, and stale liquor. A crowd of men were in a huddle at the bar, yet the barroom was strangely quiet. At the tables, glasses stood half-filled with beer, cards lay hastily abandoned, and chairs were strewn haphazardly as if some dire need demanded their occupants' departure.

Willie hesitated on the doorsill and then stepped boldly inside. Something of a powerful nature was going on at the bar, and he aimed to find out what it was.

Suddenly, like the rushing of a mighty wind through fir trees, the crowd broke apart and loud cheers and laughter sliced through the stillness. Before he could move into the midst of the men, they clustered together again like a stand of thick hemlocks. He couldn't see past the burly trunks, large limbs, and towering heights of the lumbermen and rafters. When he tried, he was shoved back. He stood on one of the chairs, then moved to a tabletop near the bar—but still couldn't glimpse whatever the crowd was viewing.

"Can you see anything from up there, lad?" a deep voice beside him asked. Startled, Willie turned to see a slightly built, shabbily dressed man with graying hair and pale eyes standing beside him.

Willie shook his head. "Not much, Mister."

The man laughed good-naturedly. "Name's Boney Quillen," he said, sticking his hand up to Willie.

"Willie Bishop, sir," Willie said, putting his hand down into Boney's and receiving a hearty shake.

"You wanna see the goin's on at the bar?" Boney said in a slow, easy manner.

"Sure do," Willie said.

"I figger I know a way you can do that, boy," the man said, his eyes lighting with mischief.

"Whatcha have in mind, Mister Quillen?"

"Well, I happen to know there be some rattlers in a box up on that there bar. If I get you up there, will you promise to touch the box of rattlers?"

"I don't have to touch the rattlers, just touch the box?" Willie asked.

"I'm telling you, that's all you hafta do," Boney said emphatically.

It seemed too easy—like Boney wasn't telling him the whole story. But so what. "I'll do it. I promise on my grandmother's grave," Willie said boldly.

"Good boy," Boney said. Looking pleased, he took a step toward the men at the bar. "I gotta fair wager for the stout-hearted," Boney bellowed.

Instantly, the crowd turned, and Willie heard several guffaws among them.

"What you up to now, you old weasel?" asked a man with wide, bushy sideburns and wild eyebrows.

"Ain't up to nothin'," Boney called back. "I just made the acquaintance here of the number-one rattlesnake champion, and I aim to wager a dirty old greenback on this fearless lad, name of Willie Bishop, iffen anyone dares to take me up on it," he said, waving a green paper at the crowd.

There was a good bit of head-shaking and laughter, but finally, one of the men with an eye gone crossed, motioned them to the bar. "If you're that eager to part with your money, Boney, well, I ain't about to stop you. Gotta warn you though, the best time tonight is forty-eight seconds, and there ain't one among us old raftsmen that can be beaten by some kid."

As Willie climbed down from the tabletop, Boney whispered in his ear. "Now you don't got nothing to fret about, son. Just march up there proud as you please and place your hand on that there rattlesnake box. Course the rattler's a little ornery, and it will strike at you, but it can't do no harm with the thick glass over it and all. All you gotta do is leave your hand on that glass for a itty-bitty minute, hardly no time at all. Those old cusses can't do it cause they been tipping too much firewater, that's all."

This invitation was much more than Willie had bargained for. He swallowed hard. How could he possibly do it when these old-timers couldn't, whiskey-sotted or not? But Willie squared his shoulders, held his head up proud, and walked with Boney right up to the bar, right up to the rattlesnake box.

Willie peered over the edge of the bar into the box. There wasn't one rattler but two, and they were slithering and hissing and pushing at the corners of the box as if trying to lift off the top. The glass didn't seem nearly as sturdy as Boney had said. It looked right thin to him.

"Them there are she-rattlers," a man beside him said. "She-rattlers are the most vicious. You stand there watching long enough, they'll git you for sure."

Willie swallowed hard. All he had to do was hold his hand on the plate of glass for one minute.

Around him came a flurry of betting against him, of money being thrown onto the counter, and the man next to him shook and rattled the box and banged the glass to keep those snakes riled up good.

Willie began to sweat. He looked around him. Abe was there, quiet, over to the side, and was looking right at him. As Willie watched, Abe fished in his pocket and pulled out a silver dollar. Dismay flooded through him as Abe threw in his lot with all the others betting against him. Boney's raggedy old dollar stayed by its lonesome.

"You wanna back out, Boney? You got money to pay all of us?" said one burly man.

Willie turned to Boney now and looked up into his face. Boney gave his shoulder a friendly squeeze. "You fellas don't understand. I'll bet this lad here's got constitution like nobody in the world has got constitution. I got a feelin' about him."

Willie thought back to earlier that afternoon

when Blanche had made him jump by sinking her fingers into his arm. Some constitution all right! A bout of dyspepsia or something of a similar, disagreeable nature whooshed through his insides.

"Heck, sonny," said the bushy sideburned man, now holding a pocket watch in one hand. "We ain't got all night while you stand there messin' your britches."

A knot of fear coiled up in Willie's stomach, and another bunched itself in his throat. He looked at the angry rattlers again and swallowed. If these men couldn't do it, how could he? But this was his big chance, the chance he had begged for, and now it was happening for real. He took a deep breath and shouted out, "Ready!"

"Go," the pocket-watch man cried. The room buzzed with talk and jeers, but Willie shut it out. He put his palm flat on the glass and pressed. He held his breath and looked straight down into the box. He watched in horror as one of the snakes reared its head. He could see its eyes, lidless and staring, its mouth wide, fangs exposed. He clamped his teeth together to keep from screaming out. He bent his head and squeezed his eyes shut.

CHAPTER 22

Willie kept his eyes shut as tightly as he could so that everything around him was completely swallowed up by darkness. He was aware of the men pressed in close around him, could hear and smell the harshness of their breath, could feel their need for him to fail. But in the darkness, the weakness and fear he had felt in the light began to disappear. His legs felt strong again, the churning in his stomach subsided.

Bang! Someone struck the side of the box, making his palm wiggle and the glass slide some. Immediately, the angry buzz of rattlers burned his ears.

Willie tensed. His fingers pressing against the glass throbbed, but he didn't budge. Thump! He felt the rattler strike the glass. His flesh crawled with the sensation of being bitten. Could the glass crack—break like thin ice?

"Yer doin' fine, son, doin' fine," the soft voice of Boney whispered close to his ear. "Just a few more seconds now."

He was going to make it. He could feel the tense-
ness begin to uncoil itself in every muscle and limb
of his body. He could feel the venom of ill will sur-
rounding him in the dead calm. Everyone else
knew he was going to win the bet, too.

"Time!" a voice called out halfheartedly.

Willie left his palm on the glass, afraid it could be
a trick.

"That'll do, boy. No need to be some kind of
show-off."

Willie lifted his hand off the glass, and only then
opened his eyes. He turned slowly to face the crowd,
and looked around at the faces mottled with drink
and anger.

From the way Boney was grabbing up the dollars
and coins tossed on the counter, Willie got the
notion that maybe both of them should get out of
town fast. His heart raced with excitement. Gawd, it
was just like being a character in a western serial.

He sidled a little closer to Boney, but there was a
sudden change in the men that caught him off
guard. Suddenly, they began cheering for him,
laughing and jostling one another in a good-
natured, sheepish sort of way.

"What a fool you've made of us, boy," said the
crossed-eyed man. "But we ain't ones to hold no
grudge. You won this here bet fair and square, and
we would be greatly obliged to yer friend Boney, if
he was to buy us all a round and a nice tall sarsaparilla for you."

"Mister, I sure could use a drink," Willie said, his legs wobbling as he inched away from the rattlesnake box.

The men laughed heartily and several clapped him companionably on the back. Willie laughed, too, although he wasn't quite certain why they were so jovial.

Abe stood and moved toward him. Willie straightened and gulped air. Abe would surely speak to him now, call him by name. But he didn't. A dark look flickered in the man's eyes; he brushed past Willie and picked up the rattlesnake box and stuck it under his arm like it was nothing at all. The men drew back and let Abe pass out of the saloon and into the night. Willie wanted to call out to him, he wanted Abe to speak his name.

"Set 'um up, bartender," Boney called. "We are drinking to this boy's future."

"To Willie Bishop," Boney said, lifting his mug high. "The bravest boy in the East."

Around the room the words were repeated, and mugs raised high. Willie lifted his own mug of sarsaparilla and drank deeply, the light in the room becoming a warm glow, blurred by the sudden moisture forming in his eyes.

"I think this calls for a little tune," Boney cried.

"A song for Willie the Kid," a voice called out.

"Here, here," the voices called out in agreement. Boney moved to the middle of the floor.

Just a young lad named Willie,
One little finger he took.
Stuck that finger in a rattlesnake's mouth
the rattler couldn't resist.
It struck right out at Willie, but
the lad he didn't budge.
And to this day folks round here say . . .
Will-lee, Will—lee Bishop
King of the Eastern Frontier.

"Git over here, boy, and sing it with me," Boney said.

Willie set his drink down on the nearest table and walked toward the center of the room. "Could I play along on my harmonica?" he asked, pulling it from his overall pocket.

"Long as you can do it nice and loud to keep us all on key."

And Willie played. It was a simple tune and no trouble at all to pick out on his harmonica. Soon, a couple of the other men were playing along on their own harmonicas, and one old man sat weeping and wiping his eyes between gulps of beer.

"Better be getting along home now, son, 'fore your pa comes looking for you," a voice nearby said.

Willie grinned. "I'll get whupped for sure if I ain't home soon," he said.

Boney walked with him to the hotel door. "Thought you might be needing some of this," he said, thrusting a handful of coins and greenbacks into Willie's hand. "You ever pass through this town again, you look up old Boney, you hear?"

Willie bobbed his head as he stuffed the money into his pocket. "Thanks, Boney, for everything," he said.

"God keep you in the right, son."

Willie nodded. "You, too, Boney."

Willie walked out across the porch and stepped down into the dirt of the street, still wondering about the goodness of Mr. Boney Quillen.

He'd only gone a short way when something white fluttering in the gentle night breeze caught his eye. On a chair outside one of the hotels lay a newspaper discarded or forgotten by someone. Willie glanced hastily around, then darted onto the porch, grabbed up the paper, and ran pell-mell until he was startled by the glow of as least a hundred lanterns lighting up the horizon.

CHAPTER 23

Willie slipped stealthily into camp. Lanterns hung on iron rods driven into the ground along the rows of crude boards crowded with townfolk. Other lanterns were hung from tall posts that lit up the stage and cast long, misshapen shadows against the curtains, making the features of Adam and the jugglers appear puppetlike and grotesque.

Willie moved cautiously toward the caravans, staying far away from the pool of the lanterns' glow. The night, Willie knew, would seem more dark to those sitting in the light. Out here, in the darkness, he would be invisible. He crouched down on the ground between Doc's and Ivan's caravans. He looked away from the murky light, away from the fluttering of a hundred moth wings against the smudged glass of the lanterns, and up at the night sky.

The wind had swept away all the cloud cover, and now thousands of tiny, twinkling stars winked at him. Fireflies flitted in the grasses and treetops, and the river seemed to murmur its pleasure from a far, distant place.

Willie wrapped his arms around his knees. It seemed as if the glow inside of him was attracting all the lights of darkness. He hummed the little song Boney had made up about him. A song of his own! A song about him! It had been a wonderful night, the best of his whole life, Willie thought, smiling to himself.

At the sound of Doc's grandiloquent words filling up the night introducing the Rattlesnake King Extraordinaire, Willie eased back against the spokes of a wooden caravan wheel and deeper into the shadows to watch.

After Doc finished, he moved from the stage down into the crowd. Abe seemed even a greater giant as he stepped out onstage in his slow, easy manner, swinging his bags of snakes. Willie leaned forward and gasped along with the crowd as Abe, so cautious at the show in Equinunk, now recklessly grabbed up a tangled nest of rattlers in each of his great hands and held them high. The big man roared savagely and waved the snakes as if he might attack, using them as weapons.

Willie could feel the hairs along the length of his arm move with a life of their own. He sucked in his breath and stood up. The shadows of the snakes loomed up against the stage curtains like monsters, like pictures he'd seen of sea serpents destroying ships in a frothy ocean. Abe would get himself killed!

"Willie!" A sharp, quiet voice cut through his trance. Willie swung quickly around. It was Doc.

Willie flinched, expecting to be struck, but he was not. Instead, Doc backed away from him into the deepest shadows, and his voice, when he spoke, held no malice. "I am grieved to my very marrow, boy. When I came to the caravan this evening, one of my flock was gone . . . gone. I was sick at heart and prevented by show preparations from following after you like the Good Shepherd. I was prepared to call you son, rely on you as a brother to my daughter—and what have you done in the first moment I leave you with her protection in my stead? Abandoned her."

"But . . . but . . . you never said," Willie spluttered.

"Where is trust, my son? Where is the fellowship between those of us who have broken bread together and wedded our words and deeds? Where?" Doc asked, his voice sorrowful, his arms limp at his sides, his chin dropped nearly to his chest. "I believed in you, son. I had faith that you were different from all those other rascally runaways in the world. Can you restore my faith? Can you pledge to be a true brother to Blanche, keep her from harm, be vigilant and steadfast, protecting her honor in a brotherly fashion?"

Willie didn't know what seized him, but he felt pressed down by a mighty hand so powerful that his knees began to buckle beneath him and he lost all will of his own. "I will, Doc," he said, overcome with the guilt of leaving Blanche alone, unprotected.

"That's good, my son," Doc said. "And God will bless you for your goodness." Doc shook himself, and the gloom that had hung around his person disappeared. He gave Willie a friendly pat on the head. "The show awaits my presence," he said. Clicking his heels, he strode off, his chest already swelling up with its customary self-importance.

Doc moved grandly through the crowd, stopping to speak to a child or to tip his hat and bow to a lady. Willie watched him, his heart growing more cold and leaden as the man moved closer to the stage. He had run like a wild, frightened rabbit into Doc's waiting snare. How had he allowed himself to be captured so easily? How?

CHAPTER 24

Just as Doc began his great speech about his medicine, Adam dropped down in the grass beside Willie.

"Mind if I join you?" Adam asked.

"No," Willie said. Apparently he wasn't nearly as invisible as he supposed since anyone who pleased had no trouble finding him. He swatted at a mosquito buzzing near his face. It squished in his fingers, and he wiped his hand clean in the dewy grass.

"Doc was looking for you," Adam said.

"He found me," Willie said glumly.

"Where were you? I was afraid you'd run off and wouldn't be back. I'm glad you're back."

Willie turned to Adam. "Thanks," he said. It was good to be missed, but he didn't feel especially glad to be back, even though it was his only hope of hooking up with Abe.

"So . . . where did you go?"

"Town. I went to town to one of the hotels and Abe was there with his snakes. It was grand, Adam." Willie broke off when he saw Blanche. She was making her way up to the front. As she stepped onto the stage, Willie felt Adam tense.

"What's she like, Willie?" Adam asked in a hushed voice. "I can't seem to get anywhere near her."

"Why not?" Willie asked, without taking his eyes off Blanche.

"I'm not sure, but I think it has something to do with the sanctimonious will of the great Doctor Granger."

"Oh." Willie had no idea what the older boy's words meant except that Doc was involved. "I bet you're right," he said heatedly.

"You know I am," Adam said. "But what is she like? She seemed different around you . . . happier somehow," he said thoughtfully.

"She's not like that girl up there!" Willie said. "She sort of treats me like I'm her brother, sort of." He broke off when some of the men in the audience whistled as she lifted her skirt to wash her feet. "They shouldn't be doing that!" Willie said hotly, his fingers balling into fists. How could Doc treat her that way? Why should Doc care if Blanche was guarded or not, the way he dressed her up?

"There's something very wrong about it, isn't there?" Adam said slowly, more to himself than to Willie. "Say, why don't the three of us visit together the first chance we can, Willie. We're the youngest ones in the troupe, you know."

"Yeah. The jugglers are older than creation," Willie said, and they both laughed.

"They're friendly enough in a reserved sort of way and glad to have a strong helper, but I don't think they fancy me as a comrade." Adam pushed his hat back as Blanche stepped off the stage. "She sure is pretty," he said softly.

Willie considered. Blanche was good-looking, though not nearly as pretty as Dorrie by his way of thinking. But he didn't say so.

"How do you plan for us to get together?" Willie asked.

This time it was Adam who shrugged. "We'll just have to wait and see," he said. The older boy left him then, and Willie watched as people rushed toward the stage to buy soap. Once again, they couldn't seem to get it fast enough. But finally, the crowd began to disperse. Lanterns bobbed through the darkness as people made their way back to town. Willie went into the caravan to wait for Blanche.

"Where were you?" Blanche cried, grabbing ahold of him when she came in. "I thought you had run off. I was afraid you were gone for good," she blurted out, sounding quite stricken.

"You wanted me out of the way, remember?" Willie said. "So I went into town."

"Oh, Willie, I didn't mean to treat you badly, I didn't want you to go away," she said, dropping his arm and backing away.

Willie took the newspaper from inside his shirt and spread it out on the table, but Blanche still pestered him.

"You shouldn't go off alone at night. Something bad could happen to you. Towns can be quite fearsome and . . . and—" Blanche paused and sat down across from him.

"And Doc doesn't want me to," Willie finished. "Don't worry, Doc already told me the good news," he said coldly.

He could feel Blanche watching him, but she was silent as he read the newspaper. He had nearly finished a feature about the decline of raftsmen on the Delaware when through the door bustled Doc with Abe right behind him.

Abe was conspicuously free of any gunnysacks. He had even removed his leather gloves and his large knuckles stood out sharply, strangely white without any cracks or redness as a lumberman's or farmer's hands were wont to have. Without his customary encumbrances, Abe seemed ill at ease, so that his hands continually sought the company of each other, clasping and unclasping nervously.

When Willie raised his eyes to Abe's face, he was startled to see him staring back. Abe nodded a greeting.

Willie nodded back, his heart starting to pick up speed like a train leaving a station. He breathed deeply and turned his attention back to the story in the paper, although he continued to watch from the corner of his eye.

Doc got a ledger from the shelf, sat down in his velvet chair, and began sorting and counting the money in a sturdy cigar box. Doc sighed from time to time and exclaimed sorrowfully about the troubles he was beset with, but Abe stood quiet and grim.

"That boy there—Willie," Abe said when Doc had finally finished his ciphering and divied up the money.

Willie jumped, surprised at the sound of his name, so strong-sounding from the giant's mouth.

"What about him?" Doc asked, his eyes flickering suspiciously. "He steal from you?"

Abe laughed. "That *would* be the first thing that came to your mind," he said. "No, no, nothing like that. Just thought you might be interested to learn that this boy fetched a powerful sum of money tonight his ownself at the American Hotel in town where I was working the bar. Course, some rascally raftsman got the money, but there might be a way to make it work for us when we move into new territory."

Doc leaned forward, his eyes darting from Abe to Willie. "What grand scheme did you have in mind?"

Willie listened with great relish as Abe related the evening's escapade. ". . . and this here youngster beat 'um all! Every last one." Abe stopped, his large frame shaking with laughter. "Never saw anything like it in all my born days."

"So what was your scheme?" Doc asked coldly.

"No grand design," Abe said. "Just a replay of tonight."

Willie smiled. The Rattlesnake King wanted him!

"I can't spare him, Abe. True, he ran off tonight,

but I was in dire straits because of his shenanigans," he said, nearly rising out of his chair.

Abe shook his head. "You've been without the boy till today. How can you feed me such damn foolishness? Why not let the boy speak for himself?" Abe paused and everyone stared at Willie.

"What do you want, Willie?" Abe said.

Willie gulped, surprised to be asked by anyone what he might favor. "Why . . . uh . . . I'd like very much to be . . ."

Dr. Granger broke in. "Now . . . now, don't be too hasty, my son," Doc said, emphasizing *my*.

Willie's excitement dropped down like the wounded rabbit he was.

"I feel I am speaking the boy's wishes when I tell you he respects your kind offer but must decline, as he has already pledged himself to other service," Doc said.

"But . . . but . . ." Willie began, feeling Doc's well-laid snare grow tighter.

Abe stepped toward the door. "Never mind, you crafty, manipulative old fox," Abe said with a disgusted sort of laugh as he lifted the latch. "One of these days, you're going to out-manipulate yourself."

Whatever Abe meant by that manipulation thing, Willie hoped that it would happen soon, because he had a notion that he would break his pledge to Dr. Granger real soon. No one—especially not Doc—was going to keep him from working with Abe.

After Abe left, Doc took a strongbox from the cupboard and unlocked it with a key that seemed to magically materialize in his hand. He put the cash in it, but before he stored the box away, he slipped some of the money into an inside pocket of his vest.

"Good night, my children," he said, lighting up a fat cigar. "The Lord will bless you for your wisdom tonight, my son." Doc fastened one of his benevolent smiles on Willie, and then went out.

CHAPTER 25

After Doc left, Blanche moved to stand behind Willie. She placed a hand on his shoulder, but he shook it off. He flicked his newspaper so that it snapped and then held it up in front of his face. But Blanche did not budge.

He wanted to be angry—he was full of wrath just like those poor, helpless rattlers trapped in a box, being teased and tormented and confused by everyone.

For some odd reason, Isaac the peddler popped suddenly into his head along with the words: "Willie, every man meets at least one Goliath in his life. Sometimes he can see the giant, sometimes the giant hides." Well, he seemed to be facing plenty of giants, and they were all fluttering around him like moths in lantern light.

"Willie?" Blanche said finally. "Did you really do what Abe said?"

Willie put the paper down and turned to face her. "Blanche," he said, "it was just like being in my own western serial!" As quickly as his anger had flared out of him, it died.

"You are much more courageous than I thought," she said softly, respect coming into her voice.

Willie looked at her gratefully. "Mister Boney Quillen made up a song about me, Blanche, and everybody in the barroom sang it. Would you like to hear it?"

"Of course," she said going back to sit on the stool opposite him at the table.

Willie pulled out his harmonica and played several bars of the song, then he sang it. The words sounded even better to him now. When he finished, Blanche clapped and cheered. "Bravo!" she said.

They lapsed into silence for a moment, Willie caught up in the warm memories of the evening until Blanche spoke. "I don't blame you for being angry about the show and everything else," she said, studying his face carefully.

"You don't?"

Blanche shook her head. "It was a mean trap Doc lured you into. He loves doing that, you know, loves to see himself as a king or god or something more powerful than anybody or anything," Blanche said hotly. "You've earned the right to work with Abe, I just don't know how we can manage it without Doc knowing." Her face became troubled. "I guess you'll be wanting to run off again. I wouldn't blame you, but, Willie, I want you to stay. Besides, it would be hard for you to work with Abe unless you stay with me. I'll help you work something out . . . somehow."

"You would? You would go behind Doc's back to help me? You would do that for me?"

Blanche nodded. "And maybe you could do one small thing for me," she said, her face coloring. "I've never had the courage to ask anyone before, never trusted anyone not to tell Doc."

Willie sucked in his breath. He'd felt from the very beginning that Blanche wanted something from him, and now he would know.

"You're ever so fond of stories and words and newspapers, more than anyone I've ever come across. I thought . . . I thought you might show me how to . . . to read and write. I've tried to teach myself, but I'm not much good," she said in a rush.

Willie shook his head in disbelief. How could a golden-tongued man like Doc have a daughter who couldn't read? "You can't read?" he stammered.

"He never wanted me to. I've never been to school. Doc's afraid I'll take up with some drifter and run off. All my life I've traveled around, gone through town after town, dressing up for the show, watching other children play together, and I had no one—no friends. If I can better myself, I might have a chance out there," she said flinging an arm toward town, "and I won't have to be trapped in this freak show the rest of my life."

Willie nodded dumbly. He understood this, how people needed different things, how he needed a life different than Nellie's. It was odd, though, how he had run away from home to join the outfit that Blanche was desperate to get away from.

"Would you stay, Willie. Please?" she asked. "For a while, at least, until you figure out what you really want to do?"

Figure out what he really wanted to do? Tonight he had, through a stroke of luck and with the help of Boney Quillen, managed to do the kind of extraordinary thing he'd dreamed of. He wanted that kind of thing to happen again.

He closed the paper, folded it up, and pushed it to one side. "If you want to learn to read, let's get started."

Blanche knelt down at the head of her bunk as if to pray, but instead she reached up along the wall and pulled out a writing tablet and pencil. "Doc's out tonight, drinking and playing cards with the others . . . as usual. At least with you here he doesn't lock the caravan like I'm a criminal," she said, coming back to the table. "He'll not worry as long as you're here, nor come back falsely accusing me of licentious behavior."

Blanche set her tablet in front of him, her face coloring again. "You can see how I've copied things down from Doc's Bible and worked at writing my letters."

Willie opened the book. Her copying was painfully neat. "I've been practicing for a long time," she said. "I burn the old tablets as soon as they are filled up. I know my numbers and ciphering, and I know which scripture is Doc's favorite because he spouts it off like days of the week. His Bible opens right up to those places. So I can read a little, but mainly I've only memorized it."

Blanche got her stool and pulled it close to him at the table.

Willie sighed. How should he begin? It was hard to remember learning to read—it seemed he always could. "Do you know the alphabet?" he asked hopefully.

Blanche shook her head.

He pointed out several letters in the newspaper and discovered that she did know most of them. He had her write down the vowels and then he sounded each one out for her, and had her do it with him. Then he took the vowel *a* and added consonants: *at*, *bat*, *cat*, *rat*, *sat*.

"You've made magic, Willie," Blanche said, her voice hushed in a kind of awe.

"You're quick to catch on," Willie said, his ears turning hot with her compliment. He was surprised by his own great enjoyment. They continued, laughing together.

"More!" Blanche said, grasping the tablet as if the words might grow legs and leap from the page like a rabbit.

They worked steadily until a knock sounded at the door. Willie and Blanche stared at each other, and Blanche quickly closed her tablet. "Don't undo the latch, just ask who's there while I put this away," Blanche whispered.

The knock sounded again. As Blanche scurried over to the bunks, Willie spread the newspaper on the table, then rose quickly from his place and went to the door.

"Who's there?" he cried out.

"Willie, it's me, Adam," the voice declared in a loud whisper.

"Adam?" Willie turned toward Blanche. She had safely hidden her papers. She nodded, and Willie undid the latch and opened the door.

As if knowing his presence might cause some alarm, Adam stepped quickly inside and latched the door again. He stood then, his hat in his hands, as he and Blanche stared at one another.

"You must be Blanche," he said.

"And you Adam," she said.

Willie looked on, surprised, as he realized this was their first meeting. "Well, come on," Willie said. "Have a sit down. Tell us what's been going on." His words seemed to break the spell.

"They've all drunk themselves into a stupor and passed out," Adam said.

"Oh, that's the way Doc's nights usually end," said Blanche.

Soon the three of them were gathered around the table, talking.

"I say, Adam," Willie said after some time. "Do tell us about where you came from."

"Yes," Blanche said. "Tell us about you."

A look of pain came into Adam's face, and Willie

was almost sorry he had asked, but it also made him all the more curious.

"I haven't had an easy life," Adam began slowly. "I lost my parents and my two sisters to cholera when I was twelve. Who can say why God chose to spare me alone? I did not wish it to be so. I had no other family and was taken to be raised by a neighbor."

Here Adam broke off, his jaw working as if he were chewing a gristly piece of meat. "I was given a place to live and food and my schooling, and I was not treated poorly but neither was I treated well. I was of no real consequence to them other than for their wish to have me work off what they felt was my debt to them for the expense of my family's burial. Why I did not run off sooner, I cannot say. Perhaps, it was only recently I deemed any debt was surely paid in full, and that I must seek a way to become a man in my own right." Adam stopped as the lamp began to sputter, and Blanche rose to fill it once again.

"There is not much else to tell," Adam said when Blanche was seated again. "But what about you, Willie? Are you an orphan also?"

Willie was suddenly awash with guilt. It poured over him in waves. He could lie or he could tell them of his early life with Ma and Pa and their wickedness to his sister, but what could he say of Nellie and Jeff that was not good? He looked at Blanche and then Adam. They were his friends. He knew that Blanche, at least, trusted him. He did not want to spoil that.

He wet his lips, and then proceeded to tell them the whole story of his life in Dyberry Forks, of how he and Nellie came to live with Jeff, of Dorrie and Thomas Thorne—and of his own unbearable longing for adventure.

To his surprise they did not receive his confession harshly, but met his story with sympathy.

"We are three lost souls," Adam said.

Blanche took one of Willie's hands in hers. "We are more alike than you think, Willie."

Willie nodded, but he was not satisfied. A part of him wanted reproach, and so he blundered on. "They don't even know what's become of me," Willie said. "If I were any sort of decent fellow, I would have left a letter. I should have done that," he said, lapsing into silence. For the first time since he left, he thought of what his leaving might have done. For the first time, he imagined Nellie pacing up and down, wringing her hands, fearful for his life, and Jefferson out searching the woods, inquiring of the neighbors if anyone had seen him. He sat as if he were turning to stone.

CHAPTER 26

The next morning, Willie woke to the sound of eggs sizzling and popping in fat and the strong smell of ham freshly sliced. His stomach grumbled loudly. When he opened his eyes, Blanche was standing in front of the little stove, cooking. She was dressed again in her checkered shirt and overalls, her face scrubbed clean of rouge, her wild hair tamed into a long braid and coiled around her head.

Willie glanced quickly around, but happily, Doc was not there. He slid off the side of his berth and dropped to the floor.

"Where'd you get eggs and ham . . . and bread and milk?" he asked, going to sit at the table. A fresh breeze swept through the window, dappling sunlight around him.

Blanche flipped eggs onto a tin plate and set it in front of him, then moved to sit opposite him at the table and watched as he filled up his plate with ham and bread. "I've been to town this morning," she said.

"Without me?" he asked indignantly.

She laughed, grabbed up his straw hat, and yanked

it down over her hair. "I pass for a young man, don't you think?" she said, muffling her voice so it sounded, well, not exactly like a boy's but not like a girl's either.

"You could," he agreed grudgingly. "Won't Doc be riled that you went to town without me? I'm supposed to guard you."

A wry smile played at Blanche's lips. "Doc doesn't care."

"Why not?" Willie scowled and made himself busy cutting up his ham.

Blanche sighed. "Doc only needs you to guard me when I'm in costume—keep an eye out for trouble during and after the show, especially the night shows, Willie. Remember the whistles and catcalls? Sometimes unsavory attentions are forced on me."

"But wouldn't Adam be better? He's older and stronger."

"He's in the show . . . and he *is* older," she said slowly, watching his face.

Willie swallowed hard as the meaning of her words sunk in. If that was the case, that meant he would never be, nor had Doc ever intended for him to be, in the show. Which was all the more reason he had to work with Abe.

"Doc expects me to keep us in provisions, and if you hadn't been snoring like an old drunk, I would've taken you with me."

This bit of news cheered him up. He took the rind from the ham and chewed it thoughtfully. "Why didn't you tell me this before?"

"I wouldn't have told you now if I didn't like you, and I don't like many runaways," she said, grinning. "They're such a nuisance." She shrugged. "Most of them go right back home if they think they are trapped here. If that doesn't work, my cantankerous nature does."

With that, Blanche stood up. "I've something for you, Willie." She turned and lifted a book down from the shelf behind her. "The way you fancy newspapers and stories . . . I had the idea that you might like to write some on your own," she said, handing him a book that was bigger than the diaries Isaac carried in his pack, or the ones Jeff cataloged his chores in.

"It must have cost a lot," he said, running his hand over the soft leather cover. This was a book intended for important events.

"Not that costly . . . not enough for Doc to get suspicious of my grocery bill."

"Thank you," Willie said. He thought of the money he had made from the night before, but somehow, seeing Blanche's pleased expression, he decided it was best not to offer payment. One day when he knew better what she fancied, he would buy her a special gift, too.

"You'll be wanting these," she said, setting a pack of pencils on the table in front of him. "And these, too," she said, giving him a couple of postcards. "We can easily post them whenever you want."

Willie could think of nothing to say, so he nodded

his thanks. He did not deserve such a friend, he thought as he looked over his gifts.

"I've got some wash to do at the river," Blanche said. "You can come over when you're done."

But Willie barely heard. Already he had taken out his pocketknife and begun to sharpen a pencil. He licked the point and began to write out the postcard:

June 22, 1888

Dear Nellie and Jeff,

I am sorry I left without a word. Please do not worry about me. I am safe and have found a job with the medicine show. We will be traveling to many towns. I will write with news again. I hope you are well.

Willie

Then he wrote the address:

Jefferson Martin
(Wallerville area)
Equinunk, Pennsylvania

Willie stared at the other card, and shook his head, but what could he write to Dorrie that would not make her feel worse over his leaving? He studied the card to his sister and then printed in scrunched up letters along the side:

Tell Dorrie I will not forget her.

Willie took his journal then. He wanted to set down all the astounding events that had befallen him since he had run away. He tried to write down his adventures as if they were part of a western serial, but everything he wrote came out in short, choppy lists resembling the entries in Jeff's journal. Nothing he wrote pleased him. Nothing was clear and vivid the way he remembered it, the way he could see it happen in his mind.

He grew discouraged after a time because of all the black erasure marks—in one place he'd even torn through the page—but he refused to give up. He decided, finally, to write down the song Boney Quillen had made up about him on a new, clean page. That was easy. And a good beginning.

He closed the journal with a satisfied feeling, and went down to the river to help Blanche.

CHAPTER 27

Several days later, Willie tried writing again. This time it went much better.

June 28, 1888
Today we left Hancock after one week being there. We traveled on to Hale Eddy, New York. Adam passed out handbills with Thaddeus and Phineas. (I finally learned the names of the two jugglers.) Me and Ivan set up the animal tent. I brushed Belle. Blanche was sewing all afternoon.

NOBODY came to the show tonight on account of there was a severe electrical storm. Doc preached to all of us in the animal tent. He said God sent the storm to cause us to rest from all our hard labors under the sun. Which he did, playing cards and drinking hard liquor with Ivan.

Me and Blanche did work at her schooling. Adam came by. It was still pouring out. We talked about our futures and ways to improve our sorry lot, which seemed pretty poor at this time, and although Adam said he has spoken to Abe about my wishes, Abe has not showed himself to me. Adam took my Hancock paper and pointed out to me and Blanche a want ad for a schoolteacher. Adam said someday he hopes to be a teacher. I took out my harmonica and played a melancholy tune. Its sad sound cheered us up somehow.

July 2, 1888

It rained for three days and three nights. Doc says God is punishing the evildoers like in the days of Noah.

We rested. Doc played cards and got sotted with Ivan, Thaddeus, and Phineas. He is using up all the profits made in Hancock says Blanche, but even though she is angry at Doc, I see she is worried, too. He will kill himself with drink, is what she says. I have been reading the Great Stories in Doc's Bible to Blanche. I read David and Goliath to her when she was sewing on her white material. I told her about Isaac the peddler and all he said to me. "A giant can be many things," she said. Blanche is very wise and catches on as quick as a rabbit runs. Quicker than me. Blanche says to me, "Willie, who is your Goliath?" In my usual way, I shrug my shoulders. I am bewildered about this. I do not know anymore. First, I thought Abe was my Goliath, but I was wrong. Now, I have to think again, so I say to her, "Blanche, do you have a Goliath?" She bites her lip and looks at me. "You know the answer to that, Willie," she says at last. She holds up the white material she is sewing on. I see now it is a dress. "Someday, I will show Doc who I really am."

July 3, 1888

No more rain. "Praise be!" says Doc. "Amen!" I adjoin. Blanche and I made more magic elixir. Adam came around and helped us as Doc made a trip into the village. We were glad to see Adam. The conversation did fill the air!

We did one show in Hale Eddy, since it is only a village like Equinunk. We moved on to Deposit. I have given up on Doc. He will never change the show. It is just as Blanche said. For all of his braggadocious talk, he doesn't give two bits about adding new acts to the show. As long as folks come, as long as he can hear his big, important self talk, as long as he sells Blanche's elixir and soap so that he can drink and smoke his fat cigars and play cards, he is as happy as a swine in a cool mudhole.

July 4, 1888

Today we camped in Deposit near the fairgrounds. There was much fanfare as it is the celebration of our Country's Independence. Me and Adam and Blanche (disguised as Blanchard!) watched the parade. The town was decorated most elaborately with flags and banners and buntings. We did have to remind Blanchard not to ooh and aah over girl things. Usually, she doesn't forget she's a HIM.

We did right brisk sales at the show tonight. Doc was most jovial and generous-spirited as he gave me and Adam and Blanche each a silver dollar. We all joined in with the townfolk and watched the fireworks together.

As usual, Doc finished his festivities of the day by card playing and drink. Me and Blanche and Adam went swimming in the river near our encampment. The moon shone full and high above the trees, and when we finished our swim, we walked along through the cemetery of the Revolutionary War heroes and an Indian burial ground. I was very solemn. I wondered were any of these mounds part of our Jeff and Dorrie's family.

I did pretend not to see Adam and Blanche holding hands in the alabaster stones. I thought long of Dorrie in her dress with the little, blue forget-me-nots. I do hope she does not forget me.

I promised myself then and there to write out a card to her on the morrow.

When we got back to the caravan, wasn't I surprised to see Abe waiting for me with his sack of snakes and special rattlesnake box. "I understand you might be interested in making a little silver if the opportunity presented itself at the right time," he says with a broad wink at Adam and Blanche. I cannot believe my good fortune!

CHAPTER 28

Willie slid away into the darkness with Abe. As it was a moonlit night and one of celebration, revelers loitered about, singing and tottering in the rutted streets still muddy and puddled from the long spell of rain. Although the night was warm, Willie shivered, deliciously, breathing in deeply, his chest swelling up with a draft of muggy air and real purpose, his back and shoulders straight—straight and tall and proud in the manner of a soldier.

Willie could not recall one single event, one memory or dream that came close to this moment of being partners with the Rattlesnake King. Surely, it would've been no small feat for a common man; surely, it was a feat bordering on the miraculous even for a boy of uncommon possibilities.

Together, he and Abe walked through the streets of Deposit to its western edge, far from the eastern side where Doc's show was camped. Abe stopped by the train tracks and the Erie Railroad Depot. Across the street loomed a row of grand hotels, each several stories high, windows shining with gaslight, porches and steps crowded still with the Independence Day merrymakers who perched on railings or sprawled in chairs, their drunken laughter and voices raised in cheerful dispute.

Willie and Abe hid in the shadow of the depot and watched the goings-on up and down the boardwalk.

Abe leaned toward him, slouching. "From here on out we split up," Abe said. "No one must suspect you might be a shill."

Willie stretched, raising himself on tiptoe to come closer to the giant's quiet utterings.

"You stay here while I go in the saloon of the Western Hotel. Wait a few minutes. Then walk over slow-like. If anyone asks why you ain't at home, tell 'um you're staying in one of the other hotels and your ma sent you to fetch your pa, and if they want to know what's his name, tell 'um Mister Smith. Go in the saloon and mosey up to the bar, and mind you, don't be looking at me." Abe paused and stared off into the distance for so long Willie feared he had changed his mind about the whole operation, but Abe turned back to him and continued.

"When you're in the bar, see how the wagering is going, and let four, maybe five bruisers back down before time is called. Then get yourself up there, close as you can, beg for a chance. Here's a silver dollar to wager," Abe said, slipping a coin to Willie. "Say something outlandish like Boney Quillen would. Then just do what you did before. Can you do that?"

Willie nodded, his breath coming short and quick, and while he was still nodding, Abe squatted, took the gunnysack and dumped, not two, but three rattlers into his special box and fitted the glass over the top.

"That glass ever break?" Willie asked.

Abe just stared without blinking and stood up.

"Did . . . did anyone ever get bitten bad or one of the rattlers get loose?"

"You ain't scared, are you, boy?"

Willie swallowed and looked up at Abe, so powerful strong and fearless of all things. He didn't want to lie to his partner, but he didn't want to admit to the truth either. He started to shrug in his usual way, but stopped. "I give you my word, I won't let you down," Willie said.

"That's good, but it's good to be scared, too, leastways a little. Ain't good not to respect these devils. I've handled these snakes for forty years and I never, ever forget not to respect a rattler. They can kill a man, and it is a torturous death you should pray never to witness. Funny thing, most men are more afeared of meeting up with a rattler than they are of ghosts or ghouls or the Grim Reaper hisself." With that, Abe picked up the box and snuggled it under his arm as if it were filled with nothing more than harmless butterflies. "Willie, before I go over there, repeat the plan to me."

If he had written down all the steps in his journal and gone over them and memorized them religiously, Willie couldn't have done better than he did as he repeated back to Abe nearly word for word what the man had told him.

Abe nodded his approval. "You're quicker than a body might suspect," he said. "I believe our scheme can cut smooth as a fresh-sharpened razor." Abe tipped his hat. "You're on your own now, son."

Willie watched as Abe, tall as a tree with a shadow long as a river, walked across the tracks, up the mired street past the Central House, past the Oquagua Hotel and livery to the Western Hotel right at the very edge of town.

Willie waited in the shadows of the brick depot, and then, with his stomach churning, his heart crashing in his chest, he stepped out of the shadows into the light of the July moon. He walked slowly, but with long strides, and fitted his steps carefully into the large footprints left in the muddy street by Abe.

CHAPTER 29

Willie clutched the silver dollar and made his way slowly up the street toward the Western Hotel, just the way Abe had said to. He took a deep breath when he came close to the hotel and stopped. He stared up at the towering wooden building and then down at the throng of men in various stages of inebriation lingering on the long porch. From inside came the sounds of a piano and a chorus of cheerful singing. In Hancock with Boney Quillen there had been no rivalry to the rattlesnake betting, but here on the Fourth of July were ominous contenders—Old Glory, Liberty, and Independence.

Old men, war veterans, dressed still in blue uniforms from the morning parade, grouped as a single regiment on the porch in front of the open saloon door. Willie moved closer, sidling past the men sitting on the steps. He could hear the soldiers talking now, talking of Gettysburg, of blood-soaked battlefields, of victory, of good friends lost. For a moment he was caught up in their talk and lingered, hoping for a story he could write down in his journal.

Catching sight of him, one soldier asked, "Can we do something for you, sonny?"

"Naw . . . no, sir," he said respectfully, and hastily moved around them and slipped inside. Willie looked quickly around. It was hard to see across the room since the smoke was as thick as early morning fog, and the room was filled with card players and drinkers and men milling about trying to get in closer to the packed bar. Willie searched the room with his eyes trying to locate Abe. He moved farther inside. A sudden commotion drew him to the far end of the saloon to the corner of the bar. A group of rough-looking men were huddled there, and nearby, on a bar stool, was Abe! Willie, his skin tingling with excitement now, inched his way across the room through the maze of tables and men.

The crowd near Abe was small, but as Willie moved closer he noticed others were joining the group and placing bets. Willie stopped at a table where several chairs had just been vacated, and now a young man about Adam's age sat drinking alone.

Willie slid into a chair next to him. "Say, friend," he said. "What's happening over there at the bar?"

"Aw, some old river man brought in a box of rattlers, but I'm no fool, I ain't going any closer than this spot right here," he said, thumping the table. "If you're smart, you won't go no closer either."

"Why not?" Willie asked.

The youth leaned toward Willie and whispered in a conspiratorial way, cupping a hand next to his mouth. "Mountain men," he said. "They love to fight for no reason. Just love to fight."

"Nobody's fighting," Willie said.

"Hah, nobody's fighting now," the young man said. "But you get wild men and mix 'um up with rattlers and wagering and somebody's gonna end up in a fight. Trust me."

Willie studied the men near Abe. They seemed to be all of a kind: barrel-chested, with legs like telegraph poles, arms bulging like boulders, faces heavily whiskered with long beards straggling down their fronts as if they'd never been touched by a barber's stropped razor. They were all dressed the same, too, in chambray shirts with collars open, rolled-up sleeves, and trousers of rough cloth held up by suspenders. Worry began to eat a small hole in his stomach, and Willie looked back at his newfound companion. "What are they doing with the snakes?" he asked.

"Aw, who knows? From here they seem to be placing bets on who can touch that rattlesnake box the longest. And from all the hollering, I can tell you, those snakes must be big and mad and as dangerous as the mountain men."

"I'd like to try it," Willie said. "It looks powerful exciting."

"My friend, have you gone mad?"

Willie half nodded. "Come on, go over with me," he urged.

"No, no, no. I don't fancy getting myself killed by the likes of them, snakes or men."

"I'm going," Willie said, getting up. The youth lunged across the table and grabbed at his shirt, but he missed and sprawled out on the table facedown.

Willie moved quickly toward the brawny men and burst with all the strength he could muster into the midst of them. He was a kid, and he reckoned that even feisty men would not hurt him.

"Hey, can I try that?" Willie said boldly.

The men drew back, jeering.

"You can try if you got the silver." One of the bruisers pounded the bar, and, for a second, the glass on the box of rattlers lifted a fraction.

Willie gulped. Those snakes were probably riled up good and desperately trying to force their way free. "I got a silver dollar, says I can do it, same as you," Willie said, opening his fist for them to see. He was very careful not to look at Abe to see how he was taking his bold speech.

"Well, come on then, put your money up here on the bar. We don't got all night, kid," one of the group said.

As if he were a magnet, as soon as he placed his dollar on the bar, the crowd in the room seemed suddenly drawn toward him to place their bets, and Willie was not surprised to see his dollar remain all by its lonesome. That was the plan. His fingers twitched greedily when he saw the pile of coins and greenbacks mounting up, coins that would soon be his.

"Get over here, young buck. Let's see how courageous you really are," the one with the longest beard said.

Willie moved into place at the bar. He looked down at the rattlers under that thin plate glass. The way their bodies were pulsing, he could almost feel their desperation for freedom. It did not take a man of considerable knowledge like Abe to see that these snakes were fiercely afraid and know that they would strike and strike and strike at anything. He marveled again at Abe's courage to hunt them and handle them, at times, with his bare hands.

"Go," a voice called.

Willie placed his palm on the glass. He had done it before, but unlike the last time, the crowd around him was noisy and boisterous. He could feel the pushing and shoving of those trying to get a better look. He closed his eyes and began counting slowly to himself, and wished to God that Boney Quillen was next to him. He counted to fifty, sixty, to seventy, and eighty. Sweat began to trickle down his face, his palms were as hot as irons heated on a stove. The snakes thumped against the glass, striking in frenzy again and again. Ninety. He counted. Ninety-one. Was it never going to end? How long would they keep him here this way, the low-down cheats? Ninety-five.

"Time," a voice called from behind the bar. The bartender?

Willie let out his breath and drew his hand away slowly and opened his eyes. Everyone around him grew quiet. He could smell the heavy breath of the whiskey drinkers and see the eyes of anger turned on him. At first, nobody said a word. Willie moved cautiously toward the pile of silver and greenbacks.

One of the men stepped between him and where the money lay piled on the bar. "Where'd you think you're going?" the man asked.

"I'm collecting my winnings," Willie said.

"No, you ain't." The man poked a finger in Willie's chest and gave him a warning push. "I don't like the looks of you, boy," he said, putting his face down near Willie's. "You've got the look of a weasel sneaking into a farmer's chicken coop. I think you're some sort of circus kid, and snakes are nothing but pets to you."

Willie shook his head and took a step backward. "They're my winnings, fair and square. I want my money!" he shouted, moving toward the rattlesnake box.

"He says he wants his mommy!" The man laughed and moved closer.

Willie placed his hands firmly on either side of the rattlesnake box. "Mister, you come one step closer," he said slowly, "and I swear to God, I will throw these devils out of this box and hurl them on you."

A gasp shuddered through the bystanders, and at this threat, most of them moved away to safety.

The man himself went white, but he stood his ground. "That could be murder, boy. You aim to kill a man for a pile of greenbacks and coins? I don't think you have the guts."

"I do," Willie said, surprised by the chill in his

voice. It was as if he had suddenly become one of the onlookers and this other boy speaking threats was someone else. He drew the box toward him. "I do have the guts, and I will throw these snakes on you if you don't give me my money."

"I ain't gonna let some kid scare me," the man said.

At that moment, a man as tall as a timber stepped in front of Willie and faced the bruiser. It was Abe.

"He *will* throw those snakes, because you've given him no other choice. Agitated as they are, those snakes will surely kill you and maybe some innocent people as well. Now, if you want to fight so bad, fight me," Abe said.

"Naw," the man said. "Just having a little fun with the kid," he muttered as he moved away.

Abe turned to Willie, his face grim. "Are you feeling tolerable?" he asked as he lifted the box from Willie's grasp.

Willie nodded.

"Collect your winnings, boy, and get yourself straight home," Abe said.

Willie grabbed up the money, stuffing the coins and greenbacks hastily into his overall pockets, and then without even a backward glance, he darted through the door and ran as fast as he could through the streets, ran with the knowledge that real danger lurked behind. When he got back to the safety of the camp, Willie dropped to his knees in the wet grass, hung his head, and vomited.

CHAPTER 30

July 5, 1888—Deposit, New York

Shortly after I returned to camp, Abe found me still kneeling in the grass where I had retched. He was most troubled over the sorry turn of the evening's events and anxious for my well-being and safety from the mountain men. He helped me to my feet and put a comforting hand on my shoulder. "You have journeyed a long way tonight, Will," Abe said to me.

"Yes, sir," I said. "I know this to be true."

I took the silver and greenbacks from my pockets and tried to give it all to Abe. I cannot say why entirely, but for some reason the sight of the money made me feel ill inside. Abe would not take it, not even a single coin. "You more than earned that money tonight, Will." His face was like the grave. I do think he knows we will not be partners again. I am not afraid to face the snakes, but the silver dollars are like stone weights in my pockets.

August 15, 1888—Masonville

I have not written in this book in such a long time

because Doc is ill and has suffered many bad spells. He will not admit this, but all of us see this and take every precaution to ease his pains in all that we do. Often he is mean and cantankerous, spewing out his great talk to hurt and malign us. We have no warning of when he may erupt, and we sit as if on Blanche's little pincushion. Only Ivan the animal trainer, who I thought was so cruel in the beginning, can seem to tame his viciousness. We are low-spirited and fear things will get worse. When Doc is resting quiet, we slip off together. Adam did say we are like the Three Musketeers, a story written a long time ago by an Alexandre Dumas. Blanche and I do not know the story, so Adam tells us all he remembers, making up the parts he has forgotten and making ourselves to be the heroes. I wish I could make up stories like Alexandre Dumas.

August 27, 1888—Windsor, New York

We have passed through many more towns, staying longer than we should in some of these places. Doc is still unwell, and his magic elixir does not work on him. He drinks more whiskey every day and becomes more vicious in his attacks. He pretends to be strong and there is no arguing with him.

This very morning, Adam told me that when we were in Masonville, he went to see about the position he found in my Hancock paper. He has been hired to teach at the Masonville School to begin in ten days. He tells me that he is taking Blanche away from this sorry life, and both of them wish for me to come with them so the Musketeers will not be separated. I tell Adam it is wonderful news. I am happy that their dreams we talked about so many times are coming true. As for me, I cannot yet say if I will go or not.

This afternoon Doc informed us that this is our last show in Windsor. Tomorrow we will go to the big city of Binghamton where he will get a fresh supply of elixir bottles shipped by the U.S. Express Company.

After Doc's announcement, Abe came to talk to me. He says he and his snakes do not like cities and his show season is over until next summer. Tomorrow he is leaving, he is going home to Kellam's Bridge. Kellam's Bridge is not far from Equinunk, he tells me. He asks if I would like to go along with him. "Will," he says. "I think you have the spirit to be a lumberman and raftsman like me." I am tempted to go. Maybe, I tell him, I will come to see you one day. But I know that I do not care to be a lumberman, any more than I care to be a farmer. I give Abe a letter for Nellie and one for Dorrie, which he promises to drop off at the general store in Equinunk. I am sorry to see Abe leave. He is a good and mighty man.

August 28, 1888

We are approaching the outskirts of the city!

CHAPTER 31

Light drops of rain began to fall as the troupe approached the city from the east. The thickening sky lent its ashen pallor to the fat plumes of gray soot spewing from the smokestacks of factories. Willie sat quietly, tensed, watching from the window, as the wagons creaked slowly across a wooden bridge spanning the Susquehanna and into the heart of this unknown giant.

The city, however, gave the traveling show not even a moment's pause. Unlike the small villages and towns where daily life came to a standstill to herald their presence, the city was bloated with its own teeming life and self-important air that comes with the explosion of progress: the squeals of the electric trolley, the commotion of construction in every quarter, the riot of carriages, wagons, and shoppers, and the shops like a cornucopia of plenty, spilling the abundance of their merchandise and groceries out onto the boardwalks along the streets. Willie tried to engage Blanche by exclaiming and commenting on the array of fancy goods and fruits that would normally catch her eye, but Blanche could not be moved from her sewing, her skillful fingers darting with a needle and thread among the folds of white material.

Willie stood watch alone as the wagons wended their way slowly along the bustling streets without stopping to post handbills or entertain passersby with juggling theatrics. Instead, Doc turned off the busy avenue into an area more sober and not without evidence of squalor.

It was here the show met with its first unpleasant surprise. As the caravans moved along the street, they began to collect vagrant children in their wake, and the passersby, instead of stopping to wave, scurried away as if in fear. It did not take long before the band of children in tattered clothes with unwashed faces had thronged alongside the wagons on both sides of the street. Their faces wore the look of the scornful, and Willie, sensing trouble, fastened in the shutters and knelt down to peer through a knothole.

No sooner had he taken up watch then the first insults were hurled at them. Along with the jeers came a rain of stones cracking against the sides of the painted wagons. Only then did Blanche put down her sewing and look up with alarm.

Willie supposed that they might all have come to real bodily injury if the law had not arrived on the scene, but with the arrival of the constable came also shame.

"Hold up! Hold up!" shouted a constable on horseback after the jeering crowd had been disbanded. The children still hung cautiously about in broken-up groups by telegraph poles, alleyways, and door stoops. The caravans came to a halt, and the law descended on Doc at the lead.

"Will they arrest us?" Willie asked.

"Nothing as tragic as that," Blanche assured him with the confidence of prior experience.

To Willie's surprise, Adam passed by and strode up to the constable. "Can't you see that this man is ill?" he asked. "If there is a problem . . ."

"We don't admit tramp shows or vagabonds in our city." The constable's chest seemed to puff out and strain against the regiment of brass buttons on his coat. "You are in violation of our nuisance codes as we require application for permits and licenses in advance of intent to sell or perform."

"Sir," Adam said. "We are in need of supplies and victuals. We cannot travel farther without reinforcements." Adam spoke with authority, his gaze unwavering.

The constable scowled, but seemed somewhat appeased by the manner and character of the young man before him.

"I will be happy to escort you safely to the city limits. You cannot enter with these wagons but if you come on foot or horseback without any intentions of selling, no one will disturb you in your transactions."

"Thank you, sir, for your kind advice," Adam said, lowering his gaze respectfully. "Now, if I may see to the comfort of this man, I would be obliged."

In a moment Adam was at the door of the caravan.

Willie and Blanche gave him a hand with putting Doc to bed. Doc's face had turned a sickly yellow and he seemed visibly shaken by this unpleasant ordeal. It was unlike Doc to allow anyone to help him, but he made no protest as they tended to his comfort. "It's only a weak spell caught me off guard. It'll pass soon enough."

It seemed apparent to Willie this was a spell not likely to pass soon, and he did not miss the quick, reassuring squeeze Adam gave Blanche.

"Willie, ride up front with me," Adam said. "I'm going to take Doc's place and lead the troupe out of the city."

With that, Willie followed him out, and climbed up on the high wagon seat. As they followed the constable through the streets, they were ridiculed and jeered at but not accosted. Willie saw plastered on the side of buildings large posters of the famous Kickapoo Indian Show—appearing at Ross Park! He was even able to catch some of the bolder print:

FANCY RIFLE SHOOTING
BY TEXAS CHARLIE

PICTURESQUE INDIAN VILLAGE

INDIAN MEDICINE CEREMONY

Introducing

GENUINE

KICKAPOO INDIAN SAGWA

When Willie pointed the posters out to Adam, the older boy nodded, his mouth set in a grim line. "Willie, no show on earth can take away our trade—it is already gone. Doctor Granger's Medicine Show is dead."

CHAPTER 32

A cold drizzle had set in by the time the troupe found a suitable place to camp outside of the city limits. The performers huddled together beneath the leafy parasol of a gracious old maple to discuss the tragic turn of events.

Willie noticed that Phineas and Thaddeus stood a little apart from the rest and expressed no sorrow over Doc's frail condition. After all was said and done, Thaddeus spoke up, "Doc has brought this sorry state of affairs upon himself and upon us all. We want what is coming to us, our caravan, and our due share of profits from the last show," he said, lapsing into silence and edging toward Phineas, who immediately took up the thread of the conversation as if they were the same person.

"And we're going to see if we cannot hook up with Texas Charlie and the Kickapoo Indian Show while they are in town," Phineas said.

Thaddeus continued, "We have no wish to be cruel to the likes of any of you, but any as would like to join us are welcome."

Ivan could barely talk. He dabbed at his eyes with a red kerchief. "How can you leave when our friend is at death's door?" he lamented. "How can you say you are not cruel?"

The pair didn't flinch from these accusations. "What about the kid? What about you?" Thaddeus said, directing his speech to Willie.

Willie looked from face to face. He saw Blanche's face freeze the way it did when something pained her, and Adam, next to her, stiffened. They exchanged looks and then turned their gaze to him.

"It's what you always dreamed of, getting to perform in a show, and few are greater than Texas Charlie," Blanche said softly. She reached out her hand and clasped his. "Willie, you've been my friend and helped me, but no one here would blame you if you left."

Willie looked thankfully at Blanche. She understood him like Nellie never had. She understood that he needed to be given a choice about things, to make up his own mind about what was best for him. "I guess I need to think on it a spell," he said.

"You can make up your mind now, or you can wait till daybreak, as we are rained in for the time being," Thaddeus said.

Willie hung his head. It was no easy matter laid out before him. What was likely to happen if he did stay? Adam and Blanche would never leave Doc in such an ailing state, they would take him back to Masonville, and he, Willie, would be just one more trouble for them.

The group broke up, Ivan following Blanche into the

caravan to sit with Doc, while Willie went with Adam to tend the horses. As they worked side by side, Willie kept his back turned slightly away from the older boy. He could hear Adam breathing and pausing, as if his friend were waiting for him to speak. But he couldn't. He needed to get away by himself for a while. He left Adam and went to sit beneath the maple in a gnarled hand of roots spreading its fingers in different directions. He leaned against the trunk. He could hear the *plip-plipping* of the rain dripping off the leaves and the aching throb of his own heartbeat.

Too much was happening too quickly, and he felt very small and terribly alone—like little David going out to face Goliath. It was as if everyone and everything—the way he knew them—were changing and disappearing. Abe was gone already; Thaddeus and Phineas most likely would be gone by the end of the day; the great Doc, who had seemed like God, had faded into a sorry shadow of a man; and Adam and Blanche were leaving in a couple of days' time for a new life. Even more mixed-up was his feeling about himself and what he should do.

Willie gripped the knots on a maple root with his hand. He could join Texas Charlie, he could work with Abe, he could go with Blanche and Adam, he could even go back to Isaac the peddler.

He sat for the longest time clutching the roots as if trying to get courage from the tree's strength. The rain stopped. The thick layer of clouds began to pull apart, letting pale sunlight come through.

CHAPTER 33

S*eptember 3, 1888—On the Erie Railroad*

Today I spent my last greenbacks for a ticket home on the Erie Railroad. I am riding in the passenger car just like the rich folk from New York City who do come to spend their summers in the country. Only I do not have a portmanteau or traveling companion. I have only my journal and my thick stack of newspapers.

It has been a most eventful week, which I am writing down herewith:

After Doc took poorly and the show fell apart, Adam informed me of his intentions to Blanche. The wedding ceremony was not much different from a church service if you ask me, and I would have nothing of interest to say about it if it hadn't been for the glorious transformation of Blanche. If I could only do a drawing or have one of those photograph inventions so that I might forever capture her as she appeared to me. She was like a delicate white rose in her dress, which she did make with her own hands, and with her lady's slippers and the pretty parasol I bought for her. Her hair was done up soft around her face in a way she had never fixed it before. I could not keep from staring at her as she bore no resemblance to the boy or the floozy she was used to pretending to be.

When the deed was done, we went straightway back to Doc, and Ivan was waiting for us, his face as long as afternoon shadows. Blanche rushed to Doc's side, and as she came near, Doc opened his eyes and a look of joy came on his face and he put out his hand. "Angel of God," he whispered. "Most blessed angel sent from God to speed to heaven the soul of his righteous servant."

Blanche held his hand, staying with him until he lapsed back in to sleep. I am sorry to say that I had to control my amusement over Doc's mistake, but did so for the sake of Blanche who was quite stricken that he did not know her when she was dressed as a lady and not in her usual manner of clothing. As it turned out, Doc never did get to know the person that Blanche really was. But somehow it seemed right that he thought she was an angel for I do think she may be.

Yesterday, we buried Doc and I confess I did shed a tear or two. I do not know if it was sincerely for Doc or for Blanche or for myself since I would be departing. Ivan was the only one overcome with grief and he wept uncontrollably for Doc, and he wept for his homeland, and for his mother, and for his brother Vassily and his sister Katrina and for many and further losses that occurred to him in the course of the day.

Blanche kindly asked Ivan to stay with her but Ivan declined. He wanted to be close to Doc. He had *found a home for his Belle at the city zoo and he had discovered many people in this city who were from his country and he could speak with them in his own tongue.*

Then it was time for me to leave. Blanche asked me to walk with her a ways while Adam was making preparations for their departure. She linked arms with me and we walked along the country road together in the warm sunshine. I did find myself choking up and so in my usual way could not speak many words. But what Blanche said to me will stay with me wherever I go. "Willie, you are the first true friend I have ever known, and in my heart will always be a special place just for you."

I did feel deeply that our promises on parting were in vain. I have doubts that we will meet again, but I do not doubt that we are friends for all time . . .

Willie looked up from his writing where he sat in the train and was met by a stony glare from an old woman in widow's weeds, her hands clasped over the crook of a cane, sitting in the seat facing him. How or when she came to be there, he did not know.

"Young man," she said, thumping her cane on the floor.

Willie looked around. "Young man?"

"You . . . young man," she said in a snippy voice, pointing the cane at his chest. "Are you writing for the papers?"

"Writing for the papers?" he asked, bewildered.

The woman in black took her cane and riffled the stack of papers on his lap.

"Besides your proclivity for parroting, do you write for the papers?"

"Do I write for the papers?" he said, his own voice sounding far away, as if he were posing the question to himself. He looked down at his journal and the stack of papers and then back at the old woman. Her face seemed to alter and become Blanche's, "I do hope you will write, Willie. . . ."—Blanche prodding him gently, praising him, seeing in him what he himself had been blind to.

"You impertinent whippersnapper," the old woman said, cracking him across the kneecaps with her cane.

"Ouch!" Willie jumped. "Begging your pardon, ma'am. I . . . I was just thinking. I . . . uh . . . I suspect that I will write for the papers one day," he said, his own words sounding a revelation in his ears.

Scowling, she studied his face. "Suspect? Suspect nothing! See to it that you do, young man."

"Yes, ma'am, I will . . . I will do it."

She sighed heavily. "Go back to your writing. You've quite wearied me with all your chitchat," she said, resting her head on the velvet seat back and closing her eyes.

When he got off the train in Equinunk, Willie sat in the station and read over his journal and pondered again the events of the summer. It was just as Abe had said. He had journeyed far. But now he knew it was only a beginning. He would go home and make things right with his sister and Jeff. And when the time came, he would leave again—leave in the day, leave without running.

When the sky changed to the duskiness of coming night, Willie rose and began the long trek home.